THE MAIN ATTRACTION

DARA GIRARD

ISBN: 978-1949764444

THE MAIN ATTRACTION

Published by ILORI Press Books

ILORI PRESS BOOKS, LLC

P.O. Box 10332

Silver Spring, MD 20914

www.iloripressbooks.com

Table for Two

Gaining Interest

Careless Rapture

Dangerous Curves

Familiar Stranger

It Happened One Wedding

Unexpected Pleasure

Midnight Promise

Sweet Temptation

Always and Forever

Truly Yours

Say Yes

Clifton Sisters

The Sapphire Pendant

The Amber Stone

The Emerald Ring

Fortune Brothers

A Tempting Proposal

A Seductive Arrangement

An Unforgettable Moment

Novels

Honest Betrayal

The Daughters of Winston Barnett

Remember My Name

Illusive Flame

Winterwood Lane

Promise Me

This Changes Everything

"I want to live with Dad."

Corinne Baylor absently looked up from her laptop screen and smiled at her seven year old son, Jason. He had a serious expression on his chocolate brown face so he must have said something important but she hadn't heard it over her typing. She was busy working on an event that had to be tied up quickly and another that was coming down the pipeline, but she had nothing to complain about. As an event planner having clients was a gift. She remembered her earlier days when she was scrambling for them. But they now kept her busy, which was why her son was eating a Pop Tart and a Red delicious apple instead of a carefully planned meal. Was he still hungry?

She glanced at the green granite kitchen counter where a stack of dishes she'd forgotten to put into the dishwasher last night sat neglected. She then shifted her gaze to the list of shopping items she needed to pick up, posted on the steel refrigerator next to Jason's picture of a purple and green monster. If he was still hungry, there was another box of tarts she'd been saving for emergencies.

Her absent smile turned apologetic before she quickly pulled a pen from her hair. It was a loosely arranged gathering of naturally tight, twisted black curls, held in place by a series of bands and pins, that the kids at school used to make fun of. Her natural hair always grew thick, long and unruly, far removed from the girls who got their hair pressed, chemically relaxed or had naturally straight hair. Because her mother had been traumatized by a hair debacle in her youth—only referred to in whispers as 'the lye disaster'—she didn't allow Corinne or her sisters to get their hair processed.

Fortunately, her mother had taught her and her two older sisters that their hair was lovely and that there was beauty in being different and to always search for advantages. One advantage that Corinne had found—or rather learned when some mean kids used to poke at her hair with straws and pencils at school—was that she could stick pens in her hair and quickly retrieve them when an idea struck her.

Moments like now. Corinne wrote down something to remind one of the vendors about a possible conflict then said, "What was that, hon?"

"I want to live with Dad."

She stuck the pen back in her hair, satisfied she'd made a note before she'd forgotten it. Okay, now Jason had said something.

Dad. He'd said 'Dad.' So at least he wasn't hungry.

That was good. She'd have to think of more breakfast items for when he returned from spending a week visiting his father, but that wasn't a problem now. What was the problem again?

Right, his father. He'd mentioned his father. What had he said again? She wouldn't force him to repeat it. She didn't want to appear as if she wasn't listening. That would be a complete parent fail and she'd done enough of those. What had he said? He wanted to do something. She wracked her brain. He'd said *I want to...*

I want to...

I want to live with Dad. Yes, that was it! He wanted to live...

She swallowed as acid filled her stomach. She hadn't eaten anything so there was nothing to make her feel nauseous. But she did.

Her heart froze as her son's words slowly, painfully, settled in her mind, calcifying in her veins, making her skin burn.

She wanted to pretend that she hadn't heard him. But she had—loud and clear. She heard him this time even though she didn't want to.

How could six words break your heart?

How could words not spoken—*I want to be somewhere else, with someone else, I'm not happy here*—hurt even more?

She could have taken anything else that Saturday morning. *Mom, I want to join the circus, I want to jump out of a plane, I want to grow up to be a mountain* (something he'd declared when he was three) but not this.

Not this quiet decision.

This painful choice.

Tears stung her eyes as she looked at the half-eaten Pop Tart and untouched apple on his plate. In the past she would have made him a proper breakfast. The apple would at least have been sliced, perhaps she would have added some scrambled eggs with shredded carrots formed into a smile. When he was four she used to make him giggle with the tree man. A pretzel stick and grape figure she used to make for him.

She was nothing like the cook her mother had been. Every breakfast had been a miniature feast, but before the divorce Corinne used to put in more effort. Unfortunately, she'd been too busy lately. Too tired most times to think of anything, let alone anything that couldn't be either toasted or microwaved. But she'd been too proud to keep asking her mother for help with cooking, although she'd offered and said it was no trouble.

Her son deserved better.

Her son wanted better.

He wanted his father instead.

She wouldn't ask him why. She could guess why and she was too afraid to hear the answer. She was a coward and knew it.

She cleared her throat and pushed some of her papers aside. She would give him her full attention. That's what he needed. That's what he deserved. They would talk this over and she'd promise him she'd do better. "Well, first we'd have to ask your father and—"

"I asked him," her son cut in, "and he said it was okay as long as you said it was."

Betrayal punched her like a fist.

He *knew?* Her ex-husband knew? He knew *first?*

That jerk! Why couldn't he have warned her that this bomb would explode in her life? That her son would choose him and his swimming pool, and gorgeous new wife over her tiny mother-in-law house and lackluster life.

Guilt that had only been a mere whisper in her life since the divorce now came out blazing, showing her all her flaws. All that she'd ruined. Her son shouldn't be eating Pop Tarts in a dirty kitchen wearing a wrinkled long-sleeved grey shirt she'd just pulled out of the dryer. She hadn't given him the life he deserved. The life she'd dreamed of for both of them. What had she done wrong? Where had she messed up?

She'd once had it all. The good job, the lovely house, and successful husband but then...but then the successful husband got restless and the fights started to happen. First small ones (how to stack the dishwasher, whether peanut butter should be refrigerated or not) then big ones (Jason's bedtime, how much Harrison spent on his third new laptop). Then ones too big to ignore (Harrison's restlessness, her unhappiness). Then there was the divorce when Jason was five. Five and full of questions as to why Mommy and Daddy weren't together anymore.

There would be no thirty-five year wedding anniversary like her parents. No steady household full of laughter and love like the one she'd grown up in. She hadn't managed to give Jason that and this was the price. She'd lost him. She'd had two years to get her life together after the divorce and she'd failed.

"School's almost finished," her son continued as if

reciting a practiced speech; she could almost hear her ex-husband's coaching, "so I can move in after that and then you don't have to worry about what you'll do with me over the summer. I know that you're worried about summer camp and—"

"It's only March so there are plenty of months left."

"But I'm doing well in school."

"And I can manage summer camp." It had been a stretch but she'd managed to reserve a spot in a prestigious program with a limited enrollment. She'd been proud of that. Fortunately, because they lived in a town with an award-winning public school system and Harrison felt comfortable with his son growing up in the same system he had (there had been only a brief discussion about private school), Corinne didn't have to worry about school fees, but she always had to be financially creative during the summer. Her parents had volunteered to help out, but after agreeing to accept their help for two summers in a row, she was determined not to use them again as default babysitters when they had busy schedules of their own.

"Dad said he'd take care of it."

Corinne gripped her hand in her lap. Of course he could. Money was never a problem for him. How typical to throw that in her face.

"And they're traveling to Italy in July. You always said you wanted me to travel."

They'd been planning it even longer than she'd thought. Her ex and Jason had thought everything through, but that came as no surprise. His father was a lawyer and savvy with arguments. He always knew how to lead a conversation, how to counterattack, she felt double teamed. She couldn't fight the logic and that was what both of them counted on.

Jason hesitated. "Are you mad?"

"No," she said in a quiet voice, although part of her was. She was mad at her ex for training their son so well, but she wasn't mad at Jason. Not at her little boy with his serious brown eyes. She couldn't be mad at him for this. She was mad at herself. Always at herself. She was to blame.

Jason licked his lower lip and looked at her expectant. "So...can I?"

"I have to think about a few things first."

Jason nodded, disappointed, and her heart ached. What was there to think about? He wanted this. He'd be better off with his father. Harrison didn't love her anymore, if ever, but he certainly loved his son.

The doorbell rang.

Usually the soft chime reminded her of the twinkling sound of happy wrens but this morning the sound felt as calming as the squawk of vultures feasting on a carcass. Her ex was at the door ready to pick Jason up for the week.

Jason jumped up.

She pointed to the Pop Tart. "Finish your breakfast. Slowly," she added when he started to chomp down the rest of his food like a wild boar.

She walked to the front door and opened it. Her temper peaked at the sight of the handsome man on her doorstep: Harrison Garrett, a man who could quickly offer charming grins and empty promises. He was a shade lighter than her own cocoa brown skin with an adorable dimple in his left cheek that still made her heart skip a beat. He took off his sunglasses, hooking them on the front of his shirt, although he didn't need them since the sun barely sneaked through the thick, sooty clouds overhead. She hoped for a downpour.

"Is he ready?"

Corinne folded her arms across her worn green sweatshirt and rested a faded jean-clad hip on the door frame. "You could have warned me."

He lifted a brow.

Corinne took a deep breath and closed her eyes. She wouldn't shout at him. That lifted brow of feigned innocence usually started a fight between them. She opened her eyes and said in a calm voice, "You're not stupid, so don't act like it."

He sighed. "I didn't know how you'd take it. What did you say?"

"She said she'd think about it," Jason said, putting on his shoes in the foyer.

Harrison gave her a long look. A look that said *What's there to think about?*

She shrugged, a wordless way of saying *A lot.*

Harrison stepped inside and grabbed Jason's backpack. Jason raced towards them pulling his suitcase. He gave her a quick hug, said, "I love you, Mom," before he dashed out the door as if he were afraid she'd hug him back and keep him there.

She felt him running away from her, keeping his distance. He was a good kid. Not one to lie. Sincere. He said he loved her.

She wanted to believe him.

But his father had said he'd loved her once—many years ago.

Corinne watched Harrison put Jason's things in the trunk of his shiny gold colored Lexus. She knew the sports car was new; he'd never shown up in it before. She was surprised he hadn't bought something more family friendly since he now had a seven month old, but that was none of her business. She and Harrison were strangers now. She'd once shared so much of herself—vulnerable parts—with this man. This man who now kept secrets from her. Who had fallen in love with another woman and gone on with his life while she felt stuck.

Nothing had changed for him. His looks, his confidence. But the divorce had left her feeling lost and empty. Her status gone. Her income slashed. The woman she'd once been had disappeared. Years ago she'd believed she was lovable and that no one who loved her would ever leave her. She knew that wasn't true.

That love could stop.

Would she lose her son's love as she had his father's? Would this loss happen slowly and then she'd be gone forever? Would she just become a shadowy figure in his life? A name but not a person? Just like she was a footnote in the life of Harrison Garrett? An ex-wife. The mother of his son. Nothing more.

In time she'd only be Jason's mom. Someone he loved at a distance but didn't care to live with.

Through a stream of tears, that slowly made its way down her cheeks, Corinne watched the Lexus speed away down the drive.

CHAPTER TWO

Jason's request repeated in her mind that afternoon as she stood on the metro's underground platform, ready to take a train downtown into the heart of DC. She was glad she'd made plans to have lunch with a friend so she had an excuse to get out of the house. She desperately needed to get out today. Even though it had been a chore to change out of her sweatshirt and jeans into a lime green blouse and dark wool trousers, which made her look somewhat more presentable.

Getting out was necessary. Not only because staying home reminded her of her son's words but because only a few feet away from her sad little life stood happily-ever-after: A lovely colonial house tucked away in a classy Maryland suburb (a suburb where you could toss a coin and hit a bank) bracketed by well tended bushes and a lush emerald green lawn. A place where a loving couple had raised their three children in comfort and love. A place of whispered *I love yous* and tender notes with drawn red hearts. Of nights by the fireplace and hugs in the kitchen.

Her parent's marriage hadn't been perfect. There had been sharp words, tense silences, twice a slammed door, but it didn't need to be perfect because there was always forgiveness and reconciliation.

Their colonial was a place where they hosted family and friends. After the divorce, Corinne had moved into the mother-in-law house, which was down a small path not far from the main house, where her Jamaican-born grandmother had died. It was a small wooden cottage painted various shades of aqua blue and had two bedrooms, one and a half baths, a sunny living room space and kitchen with a breakfast nook. Her dad, who had been an architect, had designed the small house and had it built on their large plot of land. His mother had enjoyed living there for several years.

They'd found her sitting on the couch, among the rustic wood finishes and pastel shades of the living room, with her head drooped forward and a smile on her face, a finished mystery novel on her lap. She'd had two happily-ever-afters. Two men who had loved and adored her before each of them had passed away. Corinne couldn't even manage to keep one.

Although her grandmother had died there, Corinne didn't mind moving in because there had never been any sadness. Thoughts of her grandmother only brought joy. Her grandmother had lived with such vitality. They'd thought she'd live forever. She laughed easily, made friends quickly and loved hard.

Corinne's father had the same traits so it was no surprise he'd easily won over her mother's heart.

Her two sisters had also found their happy matches. One enjoyed traveling to various countries with her long-time boyfriend and the other lived with her family in Illinois.

But not her.

Her life wasn't supposed to look like this.

She'd been given every privilege. Private schooling, travel, exposure to important social networks. But she hadn't gotten over the teasing in school. While her sisters hadn't minded being one of a few black kids in the elite school they'd attended, Corinne hadn't managed as well. The other kids found her an easy target.

Unlike many of the other girls, she was solidly built with muscular legs. The other kids called her 'thunder thighs.' After school, Corinne hated to be caught by the band members when they were practicing, especially in the hall or on the football field. The percussion section would pound the drum to mimic her steps as if a herd of elephants were walking down the corridor. If they didn't have instruments they would just say in deep voices *Boom! Boom! Boom!*.

She dropped out of track, where her sister was a star, because she wasn't very good and everybody knew it. When she lost her third race in a row, one girl had whispered wickedly, "I thought all blacks could run."

So she focused on her studies, that's where she could soar and she also worked on helping others. Her popularity soared in high school when she helped set up one of the best homecoming events in years. She was then asked to help with a festival and a winter dance. She knew she'd found her calling and a way to belong.

She earned a degree in hospitality management and quickly secured a position as an events associate at an exclusive agency. Going to an elite school had its privileges and one of her teachers had secured a meeting for her with the founder.

She worked hard and quickly rose up the ranks.

She'd met Harrison at one of the hosted events the company held for his law firm and had instantly fallen for his easy smile and compliments. He liked her laugh. He made her feel important. Desirable.

But that had been years ago.

Corinne gripped the strap of her handbag as she stared down at the metro tracks. She heard the rush of people going back and forth behind her, inhaled the scent of metal and wet coats. She walked towards the edge of the platform.

Should she try to convince Jason to stay? She had the right to say 'no', but then he'd be miserable and she didn't want that. She didn't want him to resent her.

She knew that he didn't, but then why...why wouldn't he stay with her?

She wasn't important to anyone anymore. Not like she used to be. She looked at the tunnel's black hole, it called to her in a quiet whisper. Darkness could be so peaceful. It hid so many things, covered what one didn't want to see or know about. If she took a few more steps she wouldn't have to answer Jason's question. It would be answered for him. Maybe it was for the best. Maybe he didn't need her. No one needed her. He had a stepmother.

Her.

The gorgeous brilliant one.

The confident one.

No one would miss *her.*

But if Corinne didn't come home. If she...

"That's not a good idea," a low voice of warning said.

A voice so sharp it caused Corinne to take a hasty step back, as if the voice had taken human form and had reached out and grabbed her. She spun around and saw a black man staring at her. No, glaring. His biting dark gaze pinned her to the spot. She felt suddenly exposed. As if he'd reached into her mind and knew what she'd been thinking. But why should she care what a stranger thought? Who was he to judge her?

"I have an appointment I don't want delayed," he said in the same voice. A voice that could be used for cutting through glass.

A cold, heartless voice.

"You could take a taxi or hire a driver or take the bus," she shot back, irritated by his meddling.

He nodded. "You could slit your wrists, take poison."

"What?"

"If you want to check out of life there are many ways to do it without inconveniencing others."

Corinne stared at him stunned before she stuttered, "In-in-inconveniencing?"

"Yes. Walking in front of a train would not only be a mess but others could get hurt as well. Not to mention traumatized." The corners of his mouth lifted in a slight smile. "So, I'm glad you changed your mind."

She opened her mouth, closed it then opened it again and said, "You are—" She stopped not knowing the right cutting words to insult him.

He blinked, bored. "I'm what?"

She looked him up and down. He was—in a word— beautiful. A striking, tall man with close cropped black hair, skin the color of the richest maple syrup, a hand-some face that held a certain sensual reserve. The fact that he was so attractive didn't make him any less a horrible person, which he clearly was, but calling him 'horrible' or comparing him to a donkey's behind wouldn't faze him at all.

He looked like the kind of man who'd laugh instead and find her amusing. The kind of man who'd never been teased in his life. But while he might be good looking there was a cruel elegance to him and the sound of his voice reminded her of dark alleys and bloody knife blades. He probably carried three cell phones and juggled two women who didn't know about each other. He looked as if he should be dressed in torn jeans and a too tight T-shirt instead of dark trousers and an expensive black overcoat that would protect him from the fierce March wind.

She heard the sound of the train approaching, felt the breeze as the train passed by her and settled to a stop. She stared at the rude man as he walked through the open doors, got on the train and took a seat. It was when the doors closed and she saw her horrified face reflected in the glass that she realized she'd missed her train.

CHAPTER THREE

"So what are you going to do?"

"I don't know," Corinne said relieved to have been able to tell someone about Jason's request (but not about the bastard she'd met at the metro station).

She sat with one of her closest friends in a fast-casual restaurant among the scent and sizzle of spicy chicken and mozzarella cheese sticks, staring at her untouched Cesar salad while her friend was on her fifth appetizer— baked flatbread covered in pesto. All Bonnie ever ordered were appetizers, convincing herself that she'd eat less, thus losing the extra fifteen pounds that had bothered her for years. But her strategy never worked and Corinne never had the heart to tell her. She found her friendship with Bonnie to be long-lasting but delicate.

Bonnie Divine was anything but. She was neither bonnie in nature and the only thing divine about her was the success of her family's cheap and cheerful furniture stores whose motto was 'Why settle for less when you can be Divine?'

In school, Bonnie had also been the victim of teasing. However, she did not get teased because of her name, although her name was unfortunately similar to a popular porn star at the time. She didn't get teased for her limp, stringy brown hair, which she refused to style, finding no reason to fall prey to the patriarchal idea of beauty (she'd written a paper about it). She didn't get teased for her large green eyes and pinched mouth which she colored with purple lipstick. Dark purple.

What caused devilish amusement for others at their high school was her large, jutted chin and dour personality. She was nicknamed 'The Bonfire' because she could kill any good mood with a word or a glance and could find the one stray cloud on a bright, sunny day. But Corinne overlooked that personality trait because Bonnie had been one of the few to talk to her and invite her to her house. Bonnie had helped her through her hellish years in high school and when she wasn't predicting the end of planet Earth, and possibly other planets and galaxies beyond, she had good traits.

Unfortunately, she also had the amazing ability to make anything she wore look cheap. Corinne looked at Bonnie's yellow five hundred dollar cashmere blouse and wondered why it looked as if it had come off a pile in a bargain clothes shop. But Bonnie had the money and connections enough not to care or be bothered about how people thought of her. That's what most attracted Corinne to her. She wanted to gain that kind of confidence. Bonnie had made a good life for herself. True, she hadn't had to work very hard for the managerial position in her family's business, but she was great at what she did and she had a husband who adored her.

"You know it was bound to happen," Bonnie said. She finished one flatbread then reached for another.

Corinne stared at her surprised. "What?"

"Sons are never loyal. He was going to choose his dad."

"I don't think it's that simple."

"I do. Women like us can't expect much from men."

"Women like us? What do you—"

"It's the truth." Bonnie shrugged. "I told you that marrying Harrison was a bad idea. That's why I set you up with that acquaintance of Greg's."

Corinne inwardly groaned. Greg was Bonnie's husband, a sweet man. Almost an antidote to Bonnie's more sour temperament. The acquaintance Bonnie was referring to was a guy from France with parents from Mali. A lovely man she'd gone out with a few times who 1) took delight in teasing Corinne about her deplorable French and 2) had been as exciting as dishwater.

Which had been no surprise because that's the kind of man Bonnie liked. Men like Greg who toed the line, didn't argue, kept their head down and were as sturdy as wet cardboard. Corinne, on the other hand, liked her men with a little more backbone. But, then again, Bonnie was still married, which was a win. Perhaps if she'd listened she would have been too. Bonnie had never liked Harrison.

She'd told Corinne so in no uncertain terms. She'd predicted that men like Harrison would get bored of the novelty of her (Corinne never quite understood what that 'novelty' was) before he'd trade her in for a newer model within fifteen years.

It had taken seven, but to be fair, Harrison waited a couple months before he found Lily: A woman with thin thighs and perky breasts.

At least he hadn't cheated on her. Their marriage fell apart and within two months he was looking for someone new, because men like Harrison didn't like to stay single for long and (through a happy accident?) he met a health instructor at his gym.

Naturally, Lily's job at the gym was just something she did on the side while she grew her consulting business. So Lily had beauty, brains and no baggage. Corinne couldn't blame Harrison for falling for her.

At times Corinne still wondered how she could have made things different. Maybe if she'd been smarter or something. Not sexier, she'd never be that. But she didn't like the idea that she was doomed. Although that's how Bonnie saw the world and sometimes Corinne found it comforting to share her sorrows with someone who truly understood that life could toss lemons at you and all the lemonade in the world wouldn't change things. That sometimes you had to swallow lemonade without the sugar.

Her parents didn't understand. Especially her mother who'd had a charmed life as a popular volunteer worker and stay-at-home mom. Most times Corinne felt as if she were constantly living under a raincloud.

"You won't listen to me," Bonnie said, now munching on a cheese bite, "but I'll say it anyway, let him go. If he wants to live with his father, that's it. Fighting for the affections of a seven year old is the height of masochism."

~

BONNIE WAS RIGHT, Corinne wouldn't listen. So several hours later when she met with her second closest friend, Vivian Luce, for dinner at an Italian restaurant surrounded by the scent of warm garlic bread and oregano, she was shocked when Vivian said the same.

She always ate out as much as she could when Jason was with his father, but this time she wondered if she should have stayed home.

She looked across the table stunned. "I can't believe you agree with her." She'd shared her story about Jason's request eager for a second opinion. Vivian and Bonnie never agreed on anything, which was why she kept them apart. Their one and only meeting had been disastrous.

Corinne had met Vivian only six years ago when she still worked at her old event planning agency, before striking out on her own. Vivian had been a business consultant who'd encouraged a client to use their services. Quick witted, sharp and kind, Corinne had been a little shocked when Vivian asked her out to lunch and their friendship blossomed easily.

Vivian was Bonnie's opposite in many ways. A wave of dark curls fell to her shoulders and her suits always complemented her deep honey toned skin—a mix of her Bahamian father and Italian mother. She gestured wildly and passionately in amazement when she said, "I can't believe it myself, but it's true. I know how much this must hurt, but it might also be an opportunity."

"To lose my son?"

Vivian kissed her teeth and rolled her eyes. "Don't be dramatic."

"That's how it feels."

"Maybe..." Vivian bit her lip.

"What?" Corinne pressed; it wasn't like Vivian to keep her thoughts to herself.

"It has been hard for you and remember how you worried about the cost of summer camp?"

"I can make it work. I already made the reservation. I'll slowly pay it off. Things are tight but—"

"Maybe you both need this. Don't make it permanent. Maybe just a few months. Get your life together."

"My life *is* together." But even as she said the words they felt like a lie. But she didn't know what else to do. She had a place to stay, a business she was slowly building. She didn't want to feel like a complete failure. "I need to work harder to get more clients."

"You mean you need higher paying ones so that you're not working yourself into the ground."

"It's the nature of the business."

"You wouldn't have to worry about a babysitter."

"Whose side are you on?"

"Yours. I know that after your divorce, the stress of maintaining your event planning business has been a struggle now that you're a single parent. Before, when you were married, you could afford to hire babysitters and housecleaners, but not anymore."

Corinne gritted her teeth, briefly thinking about

Jason's terrible breakfast and the stack of dishes near the sink. "I know that. My parents help out when they can—"

"But they have their own lives. You told me you've started to feel guilty and your sister in Chicago thinks you're taking advantage of them."

Her sister's criticism burned because sometimes she wondered if her sister was right. "And I clean when I get a chance."

"Which, with your schedule, is not often."

"Thanks a lot."

"You wanted honesty, right?"

"Not this honest," Corinne grumbled.

"And you're not exactly inspiring confidence in people."

"What do you mean?" Corinne said, amazed that her friend was on such a roll.

"Well you..." Vivian bit her lip.

"You're doing it again."

"What?"

"Hesitating. That's not like you. You're the one who told me that my marriage was over before I even knew it. You're the one who told me to ask my parents about the mother-in-law house when I was thinking of getting that dinky apartment. You've never had a problem telling me what you think before."

"I know, but this time it's different."

"Why?"

"I'm worried about you."

"About me? Really?"

"When's the last time you've eaten?"

"I had lunch with Bonnie only a few hours ago."

"But did you *eat* anything? You go out to eat all the time but barely touch your plate. Like now." She looked at Corinne's barely touched pasta.

Corinne poked the pasta with her fork. "I like leftovers."

"You've lost weight," she said in a soft voice. "You're not exactly thin, but you look... fragile."

"I've been working on two big events."

"I know, but that doesn't help your image. Plus..."

"What," she pressed when Vivian looked at something outside the window where streetlights shone bright in the night sky.

She turned to her, leaned forward and said in an urgent voice, "You're not *you* anymore. You don't work the way you used to when you were at the other firm. You sell yourself short. You accept clients that no one else wants, which does nothing to help build your reputation, and your business is stuck because...you've lost your passion."

Tears threatened but Corinne held them back. She wanted to say it wasn't true, but part of her knew it was. She'd take any job in order to keep her and Jason going. She wanted to pretend that she could give Jason what his father could, to not change their way of life too much.

But she'd had to. There was no cook, no housekeeper, no standby babysitter. Sometimes the cupboards were barer than she'd like them to be. That's why she'd lost weight.

She felt a warm hand on hers and looked up through tears to see Vivian's worried face. "I love you. I want what's best for you."

She pulled her hand away, ashamed. She didn't want her friend's pity. "I know."

"I think you need to think bigger."

Corinne shook her head. Both she and Bonnie wanted her to let Jason go. They were both telling her that she was a terrible mother. That he was better off without her and now she wanted her to think bigger? Think bigger about what? She felt as small as a beetle and just as valuable. "I don't know if I can."

"Of course you can." Vivian pressed her hands together as if in prayer. "I say this because I care."

"I know," Corinne said releasing a long breath. As much as it hurt, she needed to hear it. "At least it feels as if someone cares." She sniffed in disgust. "The only reason he didn't think I should kill myself was because he'd miss an appointment."

Vivian's voice sharpened. "He who?"

Corinne softly swore. She hadn't meant to say that out loud. She didn't even know why that jerk at the metro station came to mind. He was someone she definitely wanted to forget. She wondered how many hearts he'd broken both carelessly and intentionally.

Vivian held up a hand in warning. "You're not allowed to say 'nothing'."

"I wasn't really going to do it. I was just thinking about it."

"About what?"

"Stepping in front of a train."

Vivian gasped. "Corinne!"

"I know. I know. It was a moment of madness."

Vivian gripped Corinne's hand in both of hers. "Promise me you—"

"It was just a thought, but..." Her words trailed off.

"But what?"

"I don't know how he guessed what I was thinking, only thinking," she repeated seeing the horror on her friend's face, "but he told me not to do it because it would inconvenience him."

"What a shining knight," Vivian said with sarcasm.

"I know. I briefly thought of pushing him in front of the train, I doubt anyone would miss him."

"Still, I'm glad he snapped you out of it."

"He didn't do anything except ruin my day because I was only *thinking* it."

"Sure," Vivian said unconvinced. "Want me to come over?"

"I'm fine."

"Promise you'll eat whatever you don't finish here."

Corinne nodded. "Sure. Sure."

"If you ever think of doing something like that again, you'll call me first, right?"

"I wasn't going to...okay fine," she said quickly when Vivian narrowed her eyes.

Vivian pointed at her. "That's a promise you'd better keep."

CHAPTER FOUR

EAT SOMETHING she could hear Vivian telling her.

Men don't stay with women like us came Bonnie's voice.

Corinne saw herself reflected in the metro's window as the train went through a tunnel. Vivian was right. She didn't inspire confidence because she'd lost it. She'd lost her spark and fire. She'd poured everything into making sure Jason was all right, without him... what was left to care about?

She stepped off the train and headed to the upper platform, imagining her empty house then stopped when she saw a familiar older woman in a large brown overcoat struggling with a lot of shopping bags. She rushed over to her. "Let me help you," she said, wishing she remembered the older woman's name. She'd seen her at her son's school.

"Oh, thank you. I bought too much again. My daughter will scold me."

She followed the woman up the escalator as the biting March wind swept through the open mouth of the archway leading to the main level and exit, where the more leisurely sounds of suburban traffic was a welcome change to the rushed noise of the city. She looked around the parking lot. "Is someone picking you up?"

"No, I live in that apartment complex across the street. But you've helped me enough—"

"It's no trouble at all." Her parked car wasn't going anywhere and there was no one waiting for her at home so Corinne welcomed the distraction. She needed to feel useful. Once they were inside the apartment building she said, "What floor?"

"Seventh."

She'd also seen the woman around at the local park where Jason liked to play. Corinne had seen her with a younger woman and two young children.

"My name is Corinne."

"Doris."

"Do you like it here?" she asked just to be social.

"Yes, I've come to help my daughter. She is alone now."

"Widowed?"

"With luck."

"I'm sorry?" Corinne said not sure she understood. "He died?"

"No," Doris said with a laugh. "No, I only wish she were. He ran off. We don't know where he is. He was such a storyteller, promised her the sun and stars, gave her two children and then left. Poof! No word. My daughter still has hope, but I do not."

"Hmm."

"I've seen you at the school with your son."

Corinne felt her throat close. "Yes."

"And that good looking man."

"My ex."

"Ahh...I see," Doris said in a low voice filled with meaning. "At least you know where he is."

"True." It didn't help, she couldn't make up stories, she couldn't pretend that they'd get back together again. That hope had been lost long ago as well as the thought of finding someone new. She wasn't interested in romance. She just wanted the basics—keep a roof over her head, take care of her son, have food in the fridge, not run into heartless creeps at the tube station, simple things like that.

"I never did thank you for helping little Nico."

Nico was about two and had decided to strip off his clothes and run naked around the playground. Corinne had managed to capture the giggling boy and return him to his horrified guardian. "It was nothing."

"You're very kind."

She wasn't sure that was a compliment. Being kind was only something to encourage in children, adults were supposed to be ruthless and selfish; at least that's what the present media seemed to tout.

Corinne stepped into the apartment then paused, unsure she'd entered the right place. Her gaze fell on the expensive paintings, exquisite wood flooring, recessed lighting and stylish furniture.

"What did you say your daughter does?" She set the

shopping bags down with extra care afraid she would drop them.

"I didn't. She works at a construction firm. I'm lucky she and the little ones aren't home yet from their drive to Pennsylvania to visit family." Doris sent Corinne a knowing look. "You're impressed, yes?"

"It's gorgeous."

"It's mine."

"Yours?"

"Yes, I let my daughter rent it from me. I also have two other small places. After my divorce I realized that I'd never be able to retire if I didn't figure out another source of income. I was fortunate."

She had the light of spirit that reminded Corinne of her grandmother. A woman who lived life to the fullest. Who faced hard times with courage and triumphed. Doris had managed to become self-sufficient after her divorce, to be in a healthy financial position that she could support her daughter, and looked happy with her life. Corinne worried that she would never be independent and that her sisters would start to see her as a freeloader. "I want to be you."

Doris laughed. "Really?"

"You seem so together and successful and...alive."

"So are you."

"No, I'm not."

Doris took out a little black book. "Really?"

Corinne sighed. She didn't want to burden this woman with her troubles. "I'd better go."

"No, sit. Please."

She reluctantly sank into the dark green sofa surprised by how soft it felt.

Doris sat in front of her. "Who do you want to be?"

"Someone my son can be proud of."

"Only him?"

She glanced at the large flat screen TV on the wall. "I'd like to be proud of myself too, but..."

"But what?"

She returned her gaze to the woman. "It's too late."

"Look at you. You're barely in your thirties and you think it's too late?"

Corinne sighed. "I don't know how to change."

Doris wrote something in her book. "But you want to?"

"I guess. What are you—"

"You're not certain?"

"I am," Corinne corrected, responding to a determined tone in the older woman's voice. "I do want to change."

"What do you want to see different?"

"I'd like my business to be better and...I'm sorry, but what are you writing?"

"Forgive me," Doris said with a laugh. "I don't remember things if I don't write them down. What do you do?"

"I'm an event planner." She dug inside her purse to search for one of her business cards. Perhaps she could use her services one day. "Here's my card."

Doris took it and studied it, murmuring "Very nice", before she tucked it inside the book and said, "Men."

Corinne leaned forward not sure she'd heard her correctly. "I'm sorry?"

"Are you interested in men?"

"No."

"Women then?"

She shook her head. "I'm confused."

"You're not sure yet?" Doris nodded. "I understand. After a man breaks your heart it's easy to think you've wasted your—"

Corinne waved her hands. "No, I'm... You're being very kind and understanding, but I don't understand how that's relevant."

"Forgive me I should have been more clear. Would you like someone special in your life?"

"Jason is enough for me."

"And when Jason is gone?"

"I don't think I can stand heartbreak again."

"So you'd rather be alone?"

Corinne bit her lip. "It's easier."

"But what do you want?"

"I want someone I can depend on, someone I can truly trust, someone who doesn't make me feel as if they'd rather be somewhere else with someone else."

"I guess your ex taught you that."

"I don't want to make him the villain in all this. He really is a good guy but with him I always felt he wanted someone more thrilling and exciting and that's not me. I'm boring."

"To the right person you won't be. So that's a 'yes'?"

"Yes?"

"You'd like to meet someone? A man?"

Corinne frowned wondering why that would matter. "Sure, I guess."

"You only guess?" Doris said, a sharp tone returning to her voice.

"Yes, if by some miracle I could turn my business around, make my son proud, feel happy again and meet someone who doesn't find me boring that would be amazing."

The woman closed the black book with a happy grin. "I hope you mean it."

CHAPTER FIVE

Vivian had never felt so shaken.

She had been so shaken by Corinne's appearance and her thoughts of stepping in front of train that Vivian had almost missed her appointment with Brett Lattimore that Monday, but she'd managed to get herself together enough to face him.

Because facing the founder of Quest, a Washington DC property management company, always took effort.

She'd been hired to discuss possible ideas for an employees' appreciation event. Inside his wood paneled office she quickly and precisely told him different options then gave him her best suggestions and waited.

He tapped his forefinger against the desk, measuring her with his keen dark gaze before he said, "Sure."

Vivian blinked unsure she'd heard him correctly. It wasn't like Brett to agree to something so readily. Especially something Quest had never done before. She thought if she'd told him about the company hosting an awards ceremony for the employees to booster morale and cohesiveness it would be met with resistance. His last booster event, where he'd treated his employees to a special luncheon, hadn't gone well when he'd announced that he was adding to their 401(k)s rather than handing out bonuses. "They'll thank me in a couple years," he later told her. But he now wanted to do something more.

"So it's a go?" Vivian said cautious.

Brett nodded. "Yes, along with the dancing koala bears and boxing kangaroos."

She inwardly groaned. Yes, that was the response she'd been expecting. The Brett they'd all gotten used to. She'd consulted with him before and now knew when to expect his dry, biting humor. He reminded her of an ex-boyfriend—a delicious mistake with a foul mouth, five earrings and six tattoos—from her misspent youth except Brett seemed to be a little more dangerous.

There was an untamed wildness that Brett's crisp shirts couldn't hide. But for some reason although he sometimes made her nervous when she couldn't read his mood, he never made her feel afraid. Perhaps that was why they worked well together. Their first meeting had been less than ideal. Not only had she been late, she'd confused him with another client due to a scheduling mix-up because of her new assistant, and had called him by that client's name for nearly a half-hour before she realized her mistake and apologized profusely, surprised he hadn't corrected her sooner.

She'd been certain she'd made a terrible impression on him, so she'd been surprised when he'd called her again. But she was good at what she did and he always liked to deal with the best, or so he told her. "So no awards ceremony?"

"No."

"You haven't liked any of my suggestions."

He rested his chin in his hand, bored. "You only gave me three."

She stared at him stunned. "I gave you fifteen!"

"You did? Sorry, wasn't paying attention. Give them to me again." He held up a hand. "Only your top five. You know I don't like weeding through your brainstorming sessions."

He was right. She'd been in a hurry and hoped to overwhelm him with options in order to hide the fact that most weren't that good. Clever bastard. "An appreciation dinner. Spa Retreat. Outdoor team building. A—" She stopped when he pointed at her. "What?"

"I've got an idea."

She inwardly groaned. "You cannot repeat the luncheon. While your heart was in the right place it—"

He brushed her words aside. "I know. I won't do that. I want to do a training. No a workshop. Perhaps a seminar. What's the difference anyway?"

"That's suppose to booster morale?" Vivian said doubtful.

"Yes," he said, growing excited. He rubbed his chin, looking deviously sexy and pensive, which was not always a good sign. What interested Brett didn't always interest others. "Yes, that's what I want to do. They have helped me with my wealth; I want to help them grow their own."

"I'm not sure—"

"I'll share key information on how they can build wealth by harnessing the power of assets, the joys of compound interest." He pulled out a notepad and started furiously writing. "I know three people I'd want to speak and the topics that need to be discussed. I know that we won't have time to go over them all, but I'll pare it down later." He handed her the pad. "Here. Tell me what you think."

She looked at his writing and gasped in shock. "You have seventy-seven ideas?"

"No, that's eleven."

"You really need to work on your numbers. Your ones look like sevens."

"Never mind." He wiggled his fingers and she handed him back the notepad. "What do you think?" He jotted another idea down. "Maybe it could be an annual event."

He looked so excited she didn't want to discourage him. If he wanted to help his employees this way, she would help him. As a business consultant, this wasn't her specialty, but she knew an event planner who would be perfect. Corinne could use a chance like this. "I know just the woman for the job."

CHAPTER SIX

ALL THOUGHTS of her strange conversation with Doris left Corinne that Monday when she sat in her office facing Phyllis Lynde.

Corinne felt the blood leave her face. "A new color scheme?"

"Yes, silver and gold."

"B-but we've had everything set for purple."

"I don't like purple anymore. It reminds me of my ex."

"But the event is in a couple weeks."

"I know."

Corinne took a deep breath. She would not panic. She would not grab Phyllis and shake her like a rag doll. Phyllis was a woman in her fifties with two double chins she only drew attention to by wearing turtlenecks of the brightest shade she could find. Today's choice was neon pink, which matched her nail polish and eye shadow. She owned two boutique stores and had hired Corinne to host an event to highlight the clothes of upcoming designers. "We had things specifically designed for the color scheme we agreed on," Corinne said hoping to help her see the gravity of this change.

"I know."

"Then you realize that a change like this—"

"Is within my rights. I had my lawyer look over the contract and it said that a client can't make any unreasonable changes. This isn't unreasonable."

"I don't think—"

"I can also just cancel the contract and hire someone else."

"Yes. That is an option."

"But I don't want to. You came highly recommended and we work so well together. I knew it would be a pain so I made you these homemade muffins." She handed Corinne a box that smelled like something warm and sweet.

"Thanks."

She was a nightmare. A horror. A spoiled brat who Corinne hoped to never work with again, but she hoped to get referrals from this event. She could make it happen. "There will be an additional fee included due to—"

Phyllis made a dismissive wave of her hand. "That's fine. I don't care what it costs as long as it's done." She stood. "Can't wait."

"Yes."

Corinne waited for the door to close before she rested her head on the desk. She didn't know how long she stayed that way before she heard someone knock on the door. Her heart lifted with hope. Perhaps Phyllis had come to her senses? "Yes, come in."

Vivian walked into the room. Corinne's hopes fell and she rested her head back on the desk. She heard the door close.

"Should I even ask?" Vivian asked, taking a seat.

Corinne shook her head.

"I will anyway. What happened?"

She lifted up her head and sighed, defeated. "A client wants to change the color scheme. She's set on it."

"And you told her no, right?"

"I couldn't."

"Why not?"

"I need this."

"Phyllis right?"

"How did you know?"

"I just avoided—I mean—saw her. Her boutiques are amazing but the woman's a nightmare. And this is the second time she's made you look like that."

"Like what?"

"Like you want to bang your head against a desk." Vivian crossed her legs. "You don't need someone like her. Remember you had the infuriating client who gave you an ulcer?"

"Ulcers aren't caused by stress. I think it's a bacteria that—"

Vivian rolled her eyes and released a dramatic sigh. "You know what I mean."

"It's business."

"Clients like her can ruin a business. I told you that."

"I know. After her I won't do it again."

"Which you've said a hundred times."

"I mean it this time." Corinne picked up the box Phyllis had given her. "Besides, she baked me homemade muffins."

Vivian took the box, lifted the lid then frowned. "I didn't realize she worked for Dana's Donuts and More." She closed the box and set it on the desk.

"Excuse me while I swallow my pride and make some calls."

"Aren't you going to ask why I'm here?"

Corinne took out her cell phone. "Why are you here?"

Vivian snatched the phone before she could dial. "Because I have an opportunity for you. A chance to change everything."

"Really?"

"Yes." She placed the phone on the desk and clasped her hands together. "I was so excited that I left his place to come straight to you. This job will be perfect. At first I wasn't sure of his idea and then I thought if anyone could make it work you could."

Corinne frowned. "You're not making any sense. What are you talking about?"

"I'm talking about—" The musical ring tone from her cell phone stopped her. Vivian pulled it out of her pocket, looked at it and frowned. "Damn, I have to take this, how's next Tuesday for you?"

"I don't have anything planned."

"Great. Promise to keep next Tuesday morning free. Nine o'clock."

"Okay."

She pointed at her. "Promise."

"I promise."

"Great. I'll send you the details later. You'll thank me." She blew her a kiss then raced out the door. Corinne overheard her say, "Yes, yes I'm coming. Hold your horses."

Corinne couldn't stop a smile. She was used to Vivian's enthusiasm but she seemed extra excited. It made Corinne curious as to why she'd wanted her to keep the date free.

However, she didn't have a lot of time to wonder about it as she busied herself for the rest of the day calling various vendors to meet Phyllis' new demands before heading off to her second big assignment.

CHAPTER SEVEN

CORINNE BARELY MADE it through her front door that evening. Exhaustion made every step an effort. She was so exhausted she nearly missed the elegant envelope stuck between the stack of mail she'd tossed on the kitchen counter.

Was she being invited to a wedding? Please God no.

She sighed and reluctantly ripped open the gold lined envelope not caring how she destroyed the carefully designed item leaving it with ragged edges. She'd recycle it anyway.

She paused before she pulled out a handwritten note on expensive parchment paper lined with finely woven lace.

"You have been personally selected to join The Black Stockings Society an elite, members-only club that will change your life and help you find the man of your dreams. Guaranteed."

This had to be a mistake.

She checked the address and saw her full name: Charlotte "Corinne" Baylor. Nobody called her Charlotte. How had they known? This was for her? She'd been chosen? Really?

Things like this never happened to her. Was this some sort of scam? But even so there was no harm in reading more, right? What was the harm? Her life couldn't sink any lower. If nothing happened so what? She read the rest of the note. *Dumped, bored, tired of being single, ready to live dangerously?*

Corinne sagged back against the counter and took a breath, her heart suddenly racing. It all felt too close to home and surreal. Like someone had been watching her. She read the sentence again.

Dumped? Hmm...did her son count? Jason wanting to live with his father instead of her felt like getting dumped.

Bored? Hmm. Not really. Most times she felt too tired to be bored. But she felt boring. Did that count? Boring compared to Vivian or Harrison's new wife.

Tired of being single? Her heart again picked up speed. She was too afraid to answer that question. To let herself really imagine being in a relationship again.

Ready to live dangerously? Perhaps. Depends what dangerously meant. She wasn't really one for reckless partying and climbing mountains. But she could add a little shake up to her routine.

If you said yes to any question, then this is the club for you.

She tapped the envelope. Vivian had said she needed to think bigger. So even if she wasn't really ready to live dangerously, or cared about being single and was more boring than bored, she had been dumped. If there was a way to fix it she was eager to try.

Guaranteed results! Submit your application today.

Guaranteed? Really? She must be desperate to even consider falling for such a ploy. But her heart wouldn't stop racing, her hands felt sweaty. She wanted this to be real. She needed it to be. She flipped the note over, but couldn't find any more information. The Black Stockings Society? What exactly was it?

She grabbed a pen then pulled out the enclosed questionnaire, took a seat at her kitchen table and started to read.

But the questionnaire didn't make any sense. The questions were ridiculous. They didn't ask anything about her, about her goals or state of mind. How could someone be chosen as a potential candidate based on such flimsy questions?

Resigned and disappointed, Corinne stuck the pen in her hair and covered her eyes. Had her life been reduced to this? Reduced to believing in something that couldn't possibly be real? It was stupid to believe such a club existed, even worse that they'd want to invite her. She crumbled up the questionnaire and stood ready to throw it away.

"I want to live with Dad."

"You need to dream bigger."

Jason and Vivian's words gripped her.

She wanted things to be different. She wanted to attract better clients than Phyllis Lynde, she wanted her son to be proud of her, she wanted to be proud of herself.

The questions were strange, but there weren't many of them so she might as well get them over with.

She sat back down and smoothed out the questionnaire. She searched the page wondering if there was a website address where she could complete it online, but there was nothing. She took out her phone and typed in The Black Stockings Society. She found some brief sites that seemed promising but when two sent her to porn sites she stopped searching. Even the address where she was supposed to send the questionnaire didn't reveal much more than it was a local PO Box.

She either had to accept that she'd gone crazy and fill out the form or forget the entire thing. She decided to be a little crazy. She swallowed before she reread the first question.

Pets or plants?

She frowned. That question truly didn't make any sense. Why couldn't she choose both? She looked around her kitchen and thought about the rest of the house. She had plenty of plants and had never owned a pet so maybe that was the right answer. Maybe they wanted to see if she was willing to try something new. She wrote down pets.

Dragons or lions?

Was this some psychological test to measure whether she was more interested in reality or fantasy? She tapped the pen against her bottom lip. What would be the best way to answer that? She did like fantasy. She did like the thought of dragons and warlocks but that was in fiction. But going after a fantasy had gotten her in trouble. Harrison and the life she thought she'd share with him had only been in her head. Maybe it was time to be grounded in reality. Lions scared her but they were real. She had to be real too and realize there was no fantasy for her to dream about. She wrote down lions.

Snow or rain?

Ooh that was a hard one, she really liked both. Couldn't she choose both? Was that cheating? Okay, okay if she could only choose one...hmm...snow.

What is your ideal man like?

She paused before she wrote, *I don't have one anymore. I can't pretend that I can imagine any man wanting me right now. I don't see myself as a catch. I don't see myself as desirable. I'm not sure I'd trust any man who could like me as I am. I don't believe it anymore. There's so much I have to change to be better.* She paused. This response probably would disqualify her, but she wanted to be honest. As much as it hurt it also felt good. *I just want to feel like me again. Whatever that used to feel like, I'm not sure I remember anymore. I guess the ideal guy for me would be anyone who can take me warts and all. I'm not sure a guy like that exists.*

Corinne sat back and tucked the pen in her hair, her chest tight. She was being honest but she was also lying. Lying that she didn't want to eventually meet someone and share her life with him. Someone who... She took out her pen and added. *My ideal man is someone with a warm heart who could love my son as much as I do.* She tucked the pen away knowing that was a tall order, but it felt right. She then looked at the following paragraph titled: Sworn Oath. *Before signing the application please say the sworn oath aloud.*

Corinne frowned. Aloud? Did it really matter? She looked around the empty room. No one would notice. But she was one who liked to follow rules so she cleared her throat and then did so.

As a member of The Black Stockings Society, I swear I will not reveal club secrets, I will accept nothing but the best and I will no longer...

She paused at the final three words. They got stuck in her throat. They wanted her to say "settle for less" but that was easier said than done. Sometimes settling was the only way to survive. To get what you wanted. To not feel like a failure.

She bit her lip. But they were in the oath. She could say those words without really believing them, right?

I will no longer settle for less. There, she'd said it.

She quickly signed the application, paid the nominal membership fee, grumbling as she wrote down her credit card information, that it would have been so much easier if they'd used the Internet or better yet, had installed a QR code that she could scan with her phone. Perhaps if she were accepted she could make that suggestion and offer other changes. She ran outside and popped the application in the mailbox before she changed her mind.

Unfortunately, she did.

Twice.

Twice she went to the mailbox and took out the application telling herself she was not being sensible. And twice she replaced it back.

It was the second journey to the mailbox when her mother saw her.

"Is something wrong?" she called out to her.

"Uh, no."

"Come over. I know it's always hard for you when Jason's with his father." She went inside before Corinne could argue. Corinne reluctantly followed feeling newly exhausted but resigned.

CHAPTER EIGHT

Her parent's home always smelled liked spiced bun and limeaid. Her mother, perfectly dressed in a pair of black jeans and a maroon sweater set, pearl earrings that complemented her brown skin and her hair pulled back in a bun, had some waiting for her in the kitchen.

"You seem out of sorts," her mother said when Corinne sat down at the kitchen table.

Had her mother been watching her? "I just forgot a few things."

Her mother's keen gaze held hers. "Tell me what's wrong."

She didn't want to tell her. But she did with tears running down her face while her mother handed her tissues like she had when Corinne was five years old and hadn't been chosen for the school play. Once she'd finish telling her about Jason's request and her client's last minute demands, her mother sat back and said, "Well that's a right kerfuffle."

She always said that. Corinne wasn't sure her mother knew what the true meaning was, but she used the word constantly. Everything was a kerfuffle—an item sold out at the shops, a missed appointment, her daughter's life. At times Corinne imagined her mother had popped out in a London hospital looked around her and said, "Well this is a right kerfuffle" and set to tell people how to fix it.

"But we'll figure this out," her mother continued in a soft voice.

Corinne wiped her eyes. "Do you think he's right?"

"Right?"

"To want to leave me."

"I don't think it's personal, love. I'm not sure it has much to do with you."

She crumpled the tissue in her fist. "How can it not be personal? Of course it has to do with me. He wants to live with someone *else*."

Her mother patted her hand. "I'm not saying this properly. I'm sorry."

"Vivian and Bonnie think it might be good for him. What do you think?"

"I think we should ring your sisters."

"No, please don't. There's no reason for them to know about this yet. I'm asking for your opinion. What do *you* think?"

"I think you need to have a nice shower and take care of yourself."

"I'm trying."

Her father came into the kitchen and kissed her on the forehead. "You need to freshen up."

Corinne sniffed her sleeve. "Do I smell?"

"No," her mother said.

"Yes," her father countered. "Like burnt biscuits and peanut butter."

Oh, yes, she'd forgotten about helping out that evening at the second major event that had a last minute emergency due to a vendor not turning up. Corinne had had to scramble but had managed to save the event from complete collapse. "Sorry, I'll change."

"Our daughter has a right kerfuffle."

His brows shot up. "Really?"

"Our grandson wants to live with his father."

Her father pulled out a chair and sat down. "Bloody ingrate."

Her mother hit him.

He shrugged. "That's what you're thinking, isn't it?"

"Actually no," Corinne said. "I don't know what to think." Which is why I applied to become a member of a club that may or may not exist not even knowing what being a member might actually entail.

He squeezed her shoulder. "It will all work out in the end."

That was his favorite saying. As if life were some fairy story that had a tidy ending waiting to come. For him perhaps, not her. She stood. "I should dash."

"You should shower," her father called after her.

"Leave her be," her mother scolded. "She has plenty on her mind."

"She'll have a lot more on her mind if flies start following her."

"I can still hear you," Corinne called out as she opened the front door.

"If you need soap..."

"You're incorrigible," she heard her mother say with laughter in her voice.

"Or detergent," he added.

To her surprise, Corinne had a smile on her face when she left. She may not have everything figured out, but at least she wasn't alone.

THAT NIGHT she dreamed about dragons. At first she stood on the platform of the metro station and the silver body of the train slid to a stop in front of her then suddenly turned into a dragon. A large, beautiful but fierce beast that should have frightened her but only filled her with anticipation. And the dragon spoke and told her to get on board. She hesitated at first before she did, and then felt the scaled muscled back of the beast between her thighs and she rode it as it flew through the sky, taking her higher and higher.

Then she was floating and the dragon became a man. A big man with a voice like steel. She didn't see his face at first. Two other dragons, smaller in size, circled around him and they seemed playful and not afraid. He trained the dragons and they followed his every command and she watched him from a distance. Then he called to her.

"That's not a good idea," he said. "Stand by my side or you'll get hurt." She did as she was told and he finally turned to her with eyes like fire.

Her body felt hot, ablaze with heat—first fear then rage. It was him! That man from the metro! What was *he* doing in her dream? She shot awake. Her body sweaty, her breath coming out in gasps.

What an awful nightmare. How could she have been drawn to that voice? She pressed a hand against her cheek. What was wrong with her?

It was that stupid questionnaire. That's why she'd thought of dragons. But why him? He was the last thing she wanted to dream about let alone...no what she'd felt was only fear, perhaps amazement at the sight of the beautiful creatures. It wasn't attraction. She wasn't that desperate.

Her son was away. She could self pleasure. Maybe that was what was wrong with her. Pent up passion. It had been a long time and Doris talking about an ideal man had made her start thinking about men when she hadn't in years. That was it.

She fell back on her bed and squeezed her eyes shut.

It had to be.

CHAPTER NINE

She didn't know what she was expecting the following day, but the medium sized package that arrived on her doorstep wasn't it.

She didn't remember ordering anything and the box didn't have a distinctive logo to tell her who it was from. She looked at the address label and saw her name and a tiny stamp with the image of a stocking. Her heart began to pound. Could this be it? Had she been accepted into the Black Stockings Society? So quickly?

She hurried into the kitchen, sliced the seam of the box open with a pair of scissors and folded the panels back. Inside the box, encased in a purple satin cloth, were four pairs of different types of stockings, a membership card that read *Charlotte "Corinne" Baylor, Member, The Black Stockings Society.*

Her hands shook. She'd made it! They'd accepted her. She was a member. She was certain her replies on the questionnaire would have gotten her excluded but this was proof that she'd been right to follow her heart.

Corinne briefly closed her eyes and released a deep breath. One hurdle over now what?

Now that she was in the club what did that mean? Were there meetings? Would she get a listing of other members? She read the attached letter eager to find out more.

Welcome to The Black Stockings Society. Your first assignment is to take your membership card to the Wildfire Spa, where you will receive the platinum plus. Your appointment for the platinum plus has already been reserved. Please arrive at this time.

Wildfire Spa? Her racing heart threatened to stop. She hadn't gone there in months. *Years.* The last time she'd gone there she'd only been married to Harrison for six months! Jason hadn't even been thought of. How could she go back there when she wasn't that woman anymore? She'd let herself get so busy with marriage, motherhood and her new business that she'd neglected the one treat she used to give herself.

Perhaps she was over thinking things. Perhaps it was time to treat herself again. She hadn't changed that much had she? If she wore something classy she could pass for who she used to be. She went into her bathroom to see what makeup she'd need to wear, but when she saw her face she knew that no amount of foundation or concealer would work. She could not go back.

No way! She pinched her cheeks. Who was that tired looking woman staring back at her? She couldn't go back there. Nobody could see what she looked like now. Not like this. She'd been prettier back then, richer too. This sorry looking, divorced woman staring back at her was not the clientele Wildfire Spa was used to.

Corinne returned to the kitchen and frantically looked through the letter to see if there was someone she could contact. Couldn't she go to another spa? Perhaps in another city? Hell, she'd cross state lines if she had to.

But she couldn't find another option and the time she was supposed to go was...tomorrow! How was she supposed to go tomorrow? And how did they know she had nothing planned? If she missed this appointment would they take points away from her? Did the club even issue points?

But she didn't have time to write them and try to change the spa location. She chewed her lip. However, if she called the spa directly, canceled and let them know there was an unforeseen emergency, perhaps that could help her get around the predicament.

Corinne picked up her cell phone and went to their website. Since she'd been to the Wildfire Spa before she knew they allowed people to chat online with the staff. She contacted the main hub and posted: **Hello, I have an appointment scheduled for two-thirty tomorrow that I'll have to cancel. Corinne Baylor**

One moment please.

Sure.

Corinne felt her tension ease. This was going to be so easy. They hadn't even asked why she'd canceled and nobody had threatened to tell her that she'd have to pay for the missed appointment since it was at such short notice.

Ms. Baylor. Is there a reason for the cancellation?

A family emergency.

Do you wish to also cancel your membership?

Membership?

Yes, this is a special introductory offer. If you don't wish to attend we will also cancel your membership. Please repackage the stockings and leave them on the doorstep for pickup tomorrow.

My stockings?

They're part of the membership. Do you wish to proceed with the cancellation?

This was all wrong. Why were they being so strict?

Why can't I cancel this appointment and still be a member?

Those are the rules. Do you wish to proceed?

She'd lose her membership before she'd even started? What kind of club was this? And what if she'd truly had an emergency? It was if they knew she didn't.

Ms. Baylor do you wish to proceed?

She wondered if she were even talking to a human. She doubted it. **No.**

We look forward to seeing you.

Corinne set her phone down and sighed, feeling doomed.

CHAPTER TEN

Eight years was a long time.

Corinne sat in her ten year old Honda and stared at the impressive mansion, which housed the Wildfire Spa, trying to gather her courage. She had to go inside or she'd lose her membership. She'd have to walk through those large wooden doors with stain glass inlay and not look back.

A lot can happen in eight years. The spa could be under new management. Perhaps the people who used to work there had moved on. Perhaps no one would recognize her. That meant she was safe and there was nothing to worry about.

With that pep talk in the forefront of her mind, Corinne left her car and walked through the front door. Nothing much had changed inside the elegant lobby except the two clerks at the front desk. One was an older woman with fine model features and a streak of grey through her luxurious black hair; the other a young man of Asian descent with short blond hair and a black goatee. She hadn't seen them before. She felt the tension within her ease. She was safe. Truly safe.

She walked up to the counter, gave her name then handed over The Black Stockings Society membership card, which the young man swiped then stopped. His eyes widened. He handed the card back to her. "You're not supposed to be here."

"I'm not?" Had she chosen the wrong spa? The wrong day? Had the chatbot canceled her appointment after all? Was she no longer a member? "What do you mean I—"

"I'm so sorry," he said looking distressed. He hurried around the counter. "Follow me. You're on the wrong floor."

She knew the mansion had three levels but she always registered first on the main level.

Corinne followed the young man up the split staircase then down a gold and red carpeted corridor. She never even knew this part of the mansion existed and told the young man as much. "Few people know about the East Wing," he said before he led her into an elegant room where a crystal bowl filled with fruit sat in the middle of a round table and a large window welcomed in rays of sunlight. He pointed to one of the plush seats. "Someone will attend to you shortly."

The young man said the statement with such gravitas, as if she were royalty, that she wondered if he'd made a mistake. Confused her with someone else.

"Excuse me, what's your name?" she asked him.

He winced. "You're not going to make a complaint are you?"

"No, no I was just wondering if you've made a mistake."

He frowned. "A mistake?"

She tapped her chest. "Are you sure that I'm supposed to be here? Corinne Baylor."

"Charlotte "Corinne" Baylor, that's you, correct?"

She bit the inside of her cheek, unused to hearing that name. "Yes."

He grinned. "Then I'm very sure. We hope you enjoy your time with us." He left and closed the door.

This was all so very strange. Like nothing she'd ever experienced before. But that was a good thing. If she was in a part of the mansion few people knew about then nobody would recognize her. She'd get the platinum plus, whatever that was, then leave.

She picked up a red grape and popped it in her mouth, delighted by how sweet it tasted and let her tension ebb. She picked up another one.

However, when the door swung open, the second grape stuck in her throat as she stared at a familiar face—Kathleen Lafell. Kathleen had done her makeup in the past. She knew Kathleen had invented her surname, she'd told Corinne so in the past (I had to. My real name is some typical one common in my New Jersey neighborhood), but everything else about her was all real from the curvaceous figure, to the thick, brunette hair, and diamond pendant around her neck.

"Corinne?" Kathleen said, her dark gaze measuring

her from head to toe. "Oh my goodness did somebody die?"

Corinne grimaced. Did she really look that bad? "Uh...no."

"That was a joke, sweetie. Don't look so serious."

Corinne plastered on a smile. Kathleen's jokes had always been terrible.

Kathleen shook her head. "But truly, sweetie, a mortician could make you look more alive. You look terrible. I'm so glad you came to see us again. How long has it been?"

"I don't know."

Kathleen looked down at her tablet. "Yes, I have your info right here and... Oh my God that long! No wonder. Okay, what are you in here for?" Before Corinne could reply Kathleen giggled to herself and said, "Oh yes, you're a platinum plus client, just what you need. If you hadn't been I would have argued for an upgrade."

"What is platinum plus? How much—"

"As a club member it's all taken care of, sweetie."

"I hardly paid anything to apply. It certainly wasn't enough for this."

But Kathleen wasn't listening, instead she quickly took a picture of Corinne then studied the image on her tablet. "You haven't done your brows in a while." She clicked her tongue and enlarged the image. "And when was the last time you conditioned your hair?"

"I don't—"

"And that skin..." She touched a hand to her own cheek in dismay. "Did you take sandpaper to it or something?"

"It's been—"

"Your skin is just screaming for care. I can hear your pathetic little pores weeping."

"But I—"

"Never mind. That's all in the past now. You came to us just in time."

THE CREAM MASK FELT HEAVENLY. Like her skin was wrapped in silk. She felt the moisture coming back to her pores. She then had her hair washed and deep conditioned and the women were shocked at the amount of hair she had, but instead of feeling embarrassed, the way they handled her tight natural curls made her feel proud. They called her hair beautiful. The only embarrassing moment was when they found a wayward pencil stub.

"What on earth?" one of them said.

"When I'm working, it's easy to get to," Corinne explained.

"You stick pencils in your hair?"

"Pens too, sometimes."

"Stop that and treat your hair with more respect."

Once conditioned, her hair was generously oiled and moisturized before they put it in an up swept sculptured style that could be easily maintained with strategically placed hair pins. Corinne carefully watched them so that she would be able to achieve the same results at home.

After they did her eyebrows and added makeup, she stared at the mirror and could hardly recognize herself. It was as if time had been pulled back to uncover the woman she'd once been. Full of hope and expectation as if the world was hers to claim.

"Thank you for everything," Corinne said in a choked voice.

Kathleen grinned. "We're not finished yet. Now it's time for your wardrobe."

CHAPTER ELEVEN

Moments later Corinne stood in another elegant suite surrounded by racks of designer clothes. In the middle stood an attractive, full figured, dark skinned woman, wearing a red silk dress and dangling, designer gold earrings.

"Hello my name is Rania. If you have any questions, I'm happy to help."

Corinne looked at the array of clothes amazed then noticed something troubling. "Why are there mostly skirts and dresses?"

"Each one has been chosen for your size and shape and will complement you beautifully."

"But I don't wear skirts or dresses."

"You do now."

"But—I don't have to, right?" she said with a nervous laugh.

"Try them on." Rania lifted a dark blue satin dress with a thigh high front slit. "Like this."

"Unless you can find a dress or skirt with a hemline that reaches the floor I'm not interested."

"You are now," Rania said in a tone that challenged her to argue.

Corinne felt in the mood to. This woman had to be forced to understand. "No, I'm not. I don't like them. Is this because of the stockings? I know I'm supposed to wear them and I will, just under a nice pair of trousers."

Rania narrowed her eyes. "I thought you were ready to change things."

"Not like this. Are you telling me that the stockings have to be seen? I mean someone could wear gorgeous lingerie just for herself not for anyone else."

"That's true. Do you wear lovely lingerie?"

No. "I haven't had time."

"You haven't made time. Two skirts and a dress will do for now, the rest can be trousers. You don't have to wear them all the time, but it's important that you wear them at least three times."

"Why?"

"Why not?"

Corinne shrugged finding no need to argue. She could manage three days. "Okay."

"Each."

"Each?"

She nodded.

Corinne fought for patience. This woman didn't understand *at all*. "You might not know this, but I don't have nice legs. Wearing anything with a short hemline is like someone with ugly feet wearing open toe sandals."

"Prove it."

"Prove it?"

She nodded. "Try one on and let's see how hideous you are."

"I didn't say me, it's my legs."

She shrugged. "I don't see the difference."

Corinne gritted her teeth. Why was the woman being so obtuse? "Isn't there any way I could—"

Rania took a seat. "Why did you want to become a member?"

"If you read my application—"

"Repeat why you joined."

Corinne paused. There was something in the other woman's tone that warned her that arguing with her wouldn't work. "I want to do something new. Make my son proud, but I don't think showing off my tree trunk legs in a skirt will do that."

"Clothes are only an extension. There's nothing wrong with your legs only the way you look at them. I'm hoping you'll soon see that."

Corinne resisted rolling her eyes. A curvy woman like Rania oozed confidence and beauty. She'd likely never had a doubt about her body in her life. "Right."

Rania motioned to the dressing room. "Go on then."

Corinne snatched a skirt and marched into the room. She'd prove her wrong, if that's what she needed. She put on a checkered knee high skirt and red blouse. "I look like —" She stopped because she didn't see them. She knew they were there, her horrible massive thighs, but oddly they didn't look as gigantic as she remembered. She hadn't worn a skirt since high school. But the memory of 'thunder thighs' still lingered even though that wasn't how she felt. Instead She felt attractive. She liked the feel of the fabric against her skin, the soft curves of the hemline. That had to be it; the clothes were designed in a way to hide major flaws. It was all an illusion, but it worked. She didn't have slender, elegant legs but they weren't massive tree trunks either.

Perhaps this new change wouldn't be so difficult after all.

"It's perfect," Rania said when she saw her and Corinne couldn't argue. With less resistance than before, she let Rania help her select other items and started to have fun trying the different outfits on.

Rania motioned to a purple skirt and cream blouse. "This is what you'll wear to your next client meeting."

"With Phyllis?" Corinne scoffed. "She hates the color purple now, it would be a disaster."

"I'm not talking about Phyllis. I'm talking about your new client."

"I don't have a new client."

"You will," Rania said with a knowing smile.

She hadn't had a new client in months, recently her schedule had been filled by repeat clients, but it didn't hurt to dream. "Right."

"The clothes will be delivered to your house. It's a pleasure meeting you."

"So when do I get to meet the other members?"

"You don't. Not formally at least. It's not that kind of club."

"What do you mean?"

"You've likely met another member without knowing it."

"Why can't we know about each other? Why all the secrecy?"

Rania shrugged. "It's just the way the club works. Plus, it removes any comparisons. Everyone experiences the club differently to suit the changes they need to make."

"And I can't tell anyone about it?"

"No. There can be power in silence. In focusing on yourself and not spreading your energy outward, but inward."

"That's fine, but I would like to make a suggestion. Can't you set up something online or..."

"Who says we're not?"

"I checked...wait are you part of the dark web?"

"No."

"Then why can't I—"

She paused when Rania shook her head. "Too many prying eyes. We use technology and a host of different resources but not the way most members would expect us to. Writing out the application is not convenient, but that's on purpose. It lets us weed out those not willing to make an effort." She held up a hand. "Now that's enough questions. You are to follow the rest of your instructions. It's time for your journey to really begin."

CHAPTER TWELVE

A great opportunity or a big mistake. Vivian wasn't sure which as she thought about Corinne working with Brett. She sat in her office ruminating over the possibility that it could be a disaster. Corinne might not be ready and she didn't exactly inspire confidence in people. Brett could be very perceptive in his analysis of people and wouldn't take well to being part of a pity project. But she knew Corinne would be the perfect one to bring his idea to life if she believed in herself more.

Vivian lifted her gaze from her laptop screen when someone knocked on the door. "Come in."

An attractive black woman with a beaming smile waltzed into the room. She wore a fitted plaid jacket and skirt with wool tights. She opened her arms wide and slowly spun around before stopping to face her. "What do you think?"

Vivian frowned. "What do I think about what?"

"The clothes. But mainly the skirt. I never thought I'd wear one again."

Vivian frowned. Why was this woman acting as if she knew her? "Do we have an appointment?"

The woman sat down and giggled. "Stop pretending you don't know me."

Vivian reached for her phone wondering if she should call for help. This woman might be disturbed. "And should I?" she said cautiously, not wanting to upset her.

The woman looked suddenly worried. "Are you trying to be funny? Or am I bothering you?"

Her voice sounded so familiar. Especially that worried tone. It reminded her of someone...

Vivian jumped out of her seat. "No!"

Corinne shrank back, startled. "What?"

"Corinne?"

"Yes." She blinked quickly, confused. "Do I look that different?"

Different? She looked transformed. "Oh. My. God. What happened?"

"I thought I needed a change so I booked an appointment at Wildfire Spa."

Vivian came from behind her desk. "It's incredible." Vivian felt all her fears disappear. This was the kind of woman who could handle Brett Lattimore. This was the kind of woman ready to take the reins of her life again.

Corinne stood and rested a hand on her shoulder. "Don't cry."

Vivian wiped the tears away. "I'm just so happy." And relieved. She hadn't made a mistake.

"So you like it?"

"Of course I like it."

Corinne sighed and sat down again. "Bonnie said I should enjoy this new look while it lasts."

Vivian frowned. She really wished Corinne would drop her. Bonnie was always so negative. She couldn't understand why Corinne had remained friends with her so long.

Vivian folded her arms and leaned against her desk. "Unless you had a fairy godmother suddenly appear I doubt you have to worry about your clothes turning into rags."

"Right," Corinne said with a nervous laugh and she shifted her gaze away. She was hiding something.

"What's wrong?"

"Nothing." Corinne cleared her throat. "But what if she's right? What if I can't keep up this look? Bonnie thinks it will eventually be a burden to maintain. What if it is? I only look like this because my schedule wasn't busy—"

"I thought you had to deal with crazy Phyllis."

"Yes, but...I uh...really needed a break and when I saw I had a free day I thought it would be a great chance to go to the spa this time since Jason's with his dad. But when he comes back—"

"A little makeup and nice clothes aren't going to take hours. Choose your clothes and lay them out the night before. You can do this. But...where did you get the money?"

Corinne cleared her throat again. "I uh didn't. My...grandmother always used to buy me things but I never felt brave enough to wear them and I'll be paying off the spa treatment for awhile, but I just wanted to do something for me."

"Bravo." Vivian returned to her desk and grabbed her handbag. "Tell me the balance and I'll take care of it."

"You don't have to."

"You have a birthday coming up, right?"

Corinne frantically waved her away. "I really don't want you to do that." She let her hands fall to her lap. "I'm glad you're supporting me on this and not finding me frivolous. I still haven't thought about what I'm going to tell Jason when he comes back."

Vivian set the handbag down. She wished Corinne would take her offer, but she didn't want to push her. Besides, if she was able to work with Brett, the payment from that project would more than cover the cost of a little spa indulgence.

"I'm glad you came to see me so I can tell you a little more about next Tuesday."

"Yes. Why did you want me to free up my schedule?"

"I want you to pitch your services to Brett Lattimore of Quest."

Corinne blinked and didn't move. She sat so still she reminded Vivian of a robot that's central processing unit had frazzled.

"Corinne?"

"You want me to do what?"

"Meet with Brett Lat—"

"Of Quest, the property management company?"

"Yes."

"The one whose operating divisions provide property

management services to condominium associations and for rental properties?"

"Great! So you've heard of him."

"How could I not? He's been featured in *The Washingtonian*, *The Washington Post*, *The Wall Street Journal*, *Entrepreneur*—"

"He's good at what he does."

"But I've never worked with—"

Vivian returned to her desk and took a seat. "Brett may come off a little...intimidating at first, but he's a lot easier to work with than the likes of Phyllis. He's known for his charitable donations and investing in his workers so that he creates a culture that encourages productivity and wealth creation. Some employees can actually buy shares in the company. Does that sound like a scary guy to you?"

"I've never even seen his face. He's always photographed in the shadow of one of the properties his company manages, why is that?"

"He's shy about being photographed. Or perhaps he wants you to focus on his work rather than him." Vivian waved her hand and shrugged. "Who knows? It's just one of his many quirks. Nothing to worry about."

Corinne made a noncommittal sound but still looked nervous before she said, "What does he need an event planner for?"

"He's not quite sure yet."

"He's not sure?"

"He wants to run a workshop or seminar. I haven't been able to pin it down because I knew you could do a better job. He wants to expose his employees to wealth building strategies. I think talking to him more will help pin his idea down better. He isn't always the easiest to keep on target, but it's not impossible."

"And you think *I'm* the right person to do this?"

"I know you are." Vivian pointed at her with certainty. "It's time for you to believe it too. I told you I wanted you to start thinking bigger. This is your chance. Succeed with someone like Brett and you won't believe the doors that will suddenly open up for you."

CORINNE STARED at the outfit Rania had suggested she wear for her new client meeting, which she'd laid out on her bed. The rest of the new clothes she'd put away in her closet. But this outfit took all her attention.

How had they known?

She turned to the full length mirror standing in the corner and stared at the woman who had left the Wildfire Spa only a few hours ago. A woman who looked attractive and successful. She didn't want this feeling to end. She knew it would eventually. Soon she'd have to wipe off the makeup and tie up her hair and get into her worn pajamas. She'd be the ordinary Corinne again.

I will not settle for less.

That's the part of the oath Rania had had her repeat before Corinne left. Things had changed. She had to believe it. Starting tomorrow she wouldn't race through her morning. She'd take care of herself.

If she didn't want this feeling to end she'd have to fight to keep it. Even the instructions had told her that she had to wear one of her new stockings to the meeting next Tuesday.

A meeting with the founder of Quest.

She didn't know which one to choose. The four stockings weren't too shocking, but they all seemed more daring than anything she would have chosen. She decided on a latticed patterned one. Since he liked buildings, perhaps a cross pattern would work with him. Not that she expected him to be looking at her legs, heaven forbid, but it seemed the most suitable.

She couldn't believe Vivian had gotten this chance for her. She was to pitch her services to Brett Lattimore. The man in the shadows.

She'd never thought she'd have Quest as a possible client, let alone work with a man who liked to be anonymous. She'd never have thought of approaching a company like his. Could she do this?

She had to try.

She didn't want to let Vivian down. She believed in her. This was her chance. Even if he turned her down, at least she'd give it her best. No more settling.

But first she'd have to give Jason his answer.

CHAPTER THIRTEEN

"Six months?" Jason and Harrison said in unison.

When Harrison had returned that Saturday to drop Jason off, she'd invited them to sit in the living room to tell them her decision.

"Yes," she said. "Just as a trial. Six months with your father and then six months with me. I don't want to make any rash long-term decisions right now. Six months or nothing."

Jason looked at his father for guidance. Harrison shrugged. "Sounds fair."

"But I also want to have a full weekend with you once a month. Okay?"

Jason shrugged.

Harrison nodded and spoke for his son. "That's fine."

"So I can pack up now?"

Corinne swallowed, hurt that he was still so eager to leave. "If you want."

"Okay." He looked at his father. "Can I get a couple more things?"

"Sure. Need help?"

"No." He raced out of the room.

Harrison returned his gaze to her. "I know how hard this is for you."

Corinne flexed her hands in her lap determined to keep herself in check. She'd fall apart when they left. Jason still wanted to go. He wanted to be away from her. "I doubt it."

Harrison leaned back against the couch cushions and studied her with appreciation. "So what has gotten into you?"

"What do you mean?"

A teasing smile touched his lips. "You know exactly what I mean." He looked her up and down. "I've never seen you like this before. The hair, the clothes. You look amazing."

Corinne felt her face grow warm. A compliment from her ex shouldn't make her so happy, but it did. More than she wanted to admit. That morning she had made sure to wear makeup and a new red blouse. "I thought it was time for a change."

"I hope you won't be disappointed though."

"Disappointed?"

"If this scheme doesn't work."

"Scheme?"

"Yes, splitting his time between us. If at the end of it all he still wants to live with me, you will be okay with that, right?"

No, but she'd have to accept it. "I don't want to think

about the future right now. Making this decision is hard enough."

Harrison nodded in understanding. "I know." He grinned before he winked, reminding her of when he used to flirt with her. "I'm a little jealous."

"Jealous?"

"That you never made an effort like this for me."

Corinne stiffened, sensing criticism. "I had but you hadn't noticed."

"Trust me, if you'd done something like this, I would have noticed."

"Maybe." Probably. Perhaps if she'd gotten an invitation to The Black Stockings Society sooner she could have saved her marriage. She stood, not wanting to reflect on the past and think about what she couldn't fix. It was too late to win him back. "I'm going to check on Jason."

SHE FOUND him in his bedroom stuffing an action figure in a duffle bag. "I have another packing box for you," she said setting it on the bed.

"Thanks."

She looked at pictures of The Hulk, Cyborg and Black Panther hanging on his wall. "Do you want me to help you take down the posters?"

"No," he said in a soft voice as he put a stuffed bear in the bag.

She sensed he was avoiding her gaze, but couldn't understand why. She didn't want to pressure him. "I'll miss you."

"Hmm."

Since he was so focused on taking his toys she did the adult thing and got another suitcase and packed more clothes, his shoes, and the items he'd need for his after-school art class. She closed the lid of the box and zipped up the suitcase with a sigh. The room still had enough items to remind her that it was his whenever he needed it, that she would get to see him one weekend a month, but it still felt empty. She blinked back tears and grabbed the box. "I'll come back for the suitcase, it's heavy," she said.

She helped Harrison pack Jason's items in the trunk, before she turned and squeezed Jason on the shoulder, sensing he wanted to keep his distance from her, but he surprised her with a quick hug and whispered, "You look pretty," before he darted into the backseat and closed the door.

She didn't cry as she watched the Lexus drive away. She didn't know how to take his quiet words, when he'd barely been able to look at her.

One day she'd get him to. One day she'd make him laugh again, one day he'd be the carefree kid she knew and loved. She gripped her hand into a fist. One day she would win him back.

She heard footsteps hurrying across the grass and turned and saw her mother coming towards her. "Was that Harrison?"

"Yes,"

"I saw you packing things in the trunk. Does this mean...?"

Corinne took a deep breath. She'd made her decision

and would stand by it. "Jason's staying with his father a little longer as a trial run."

"Have you eaten? Do you want to come over for dinner?"

Corinne plastered on a smile. "I'm fine, Mom."

Her mother took her hand and led her towards Corinne's front door. "Let's go inside."

"Mom, I really don't—"

"I won't force you to eat anything. I only need a quick chat." Corinne let her mother drag her into the living room and sat down before she said, "What is it?"

Her mother sat in front of her and pressed her hands together. "Oh dear. How do I say this?"

Corinne folded her arms and sighed. "Mom, please just—"

"I'm afraid this strategy isn't the best one."

"Strategy?"

"You are an attractive woman, but it's not the only way to handle men."

"I don't know what you're talking about."

"I know he's your ex, but that doesn't change anything. He's a married man now."

Corinne frowned. "I *still* don't know what you're talking about."

She licked her lower lip and rubbed her forehead. "What a terrible kerfuffle."

"Mum!" Corinne said, using a word she only said when she was annoyed.

"I know you're desperate, but trying to seduce Harrison—"

"What!"

"Is a bit overboard."

Corinne stared at her shocked. "S-seduce? I'm not trying to seduce anyone."

"But your hair and clothes. You haven't dressed like this in years. You suddenly decide to get a makeover when Jason wants to live with his father. What does that mean?"

"My makeover has nothing to do with seducing Harrison. I thought you had a better opinion of me."

"What else was I to think? Your sisters have tried for years to get you to dress up a bit and you've refused. What's different now?"

I joined a secret club. But she couldn't tell her that. She couldn't tell anyone. "I have a new client I have to impress. I thought this new look would help me with my business."

Her mother motioned to her makeup and clothes. "So all this is for business?"

No. "Yes."

Her mother released a sigh of relief. "Well, in that case you look sensational."

Corinne stood feeling suddenly tired. Bonnie thought the makeover wouldn't last, Vivian thought it could help her win a new client, her ex-husband thought she was trying to win back their son and her mother thought she was trying to seduce her ex. It was all too much. She wanted to be alone. "Thanks."

Her mother kissed her on the cheek and she smelled liked ginger. "Now I can tell your father not to worry either."

"I can't believe you two—"

"If you saw it from our perspective you'd understand. One day you leave the house looking like a drowned rat—"

"Mum!"

"And come back looking like a sex kitten."

Corinne shook her head. "Not exactly."

Her mother grinned. "But I'm close."

"Maybe you should stop watching me."

"You're our daughter. That will never happen."

Corinne hurried her mother out of the house then sat alone in the kitchen. She'd done it.

She'd made a decision about Jason.

She'd taken a risk and joined a secret club.

She'd agreed to pitch her services to a new client.

Now all she had to do was win him over.

For the first time in years, she wasn't afraid, she was excited.

CHAPTER FOURTEEN

She felt surprisingly calm as she rode the metro for her meeting at Quest's downtown office. But as she hurried through the crowded platform she bumped into someone and dropped her portfolio. "Oh, I'm sorry," she said, but before she could reach for it a strong brown hand held the portfolio out to her. "Glad to see you're still with us."

She froze. She knew that voice. That cuttingly cruel voice.

The Neanderthal! Her eyes flew up and she saw that aggravatingly beautiful face. She gasped. What were the odds of bumping into him again? What was he doing there?! Why did he have to be at this station? She snatched the portfolio from him. The handle felt hot from his touch. As if he'd just traveled up from Hades to torment her.

Fortunately, his comment had been too low for others

to hear, not that anyone would have understood his cryptic message if they had.

Meeting him again had been unlucky, but she wouldn't let him rattle her. She was prepared for this. The makeover, the stockings, she'd win over the founder of Quest and then win Jason back. He'd see the kind of mother he had. She was no pushover, she was a winner. Corinne opened her mouth to make a rude reply, but he didn't give her a chance. He turned and walked away.

She stared at his broad back wanting to create as much distance between them as she could.

Unfortunately, after watching him head to the station's east exit and up the escalators she had a sinking feeling that she'd have to stay behind him longer than she'd hoped because he seemed to be going in the same direction she was. Once they left the station and headed down the sidewalk she kept waiting for him to cross the street, turn into an alleyway, disappear into a building. But he didn't.

She sighed resigned. Since he wasn't going anywhere and his broad, erect posture stood out among the crush of people hurrying back and forth, she took a moment to watch how he walked. He didn't just walk, he *moved*. His causal gait propelled him forward with a masculine grace she'd rarely seen. Even when she wanted to look away, her gaze kept returning to him as if it almost demanded her to.

She'd been studying him with such intent that it took her a few moments to realize that he'd arrived at his destination when she followed him through the glass doors to one of the elevators.

She paused and hastily raced out of the building. What was wrong with her? At least he hadn't turned around and seen her. That would have been embarrassing. She gripped her chest and took a deep breath. Now that he was gone she could focus. First she had to figure out where she was. She looked up at the street address on the side of the building.

Wait. This was *her* building. The building where she was supposed to have the meeting. What were the odds? Corinne paused and checked the address just to make sure. There were a number of offices inside. It was probably just an awful coincidence. When she stepped inside she was relieved to see that the man was nowhere in sight.

No, it was impossible. It couldn't be him.

She laughed at her foolishness. That would be a nightmare and Vivian had told her that he wasn't scary. That his employees liked him. No one could like that bastard.

Corinne took the elevator and walked into the conference room ready to take charge. She paused when she saw three figures. Two women and a man.

A Neanderthal dressed in an ice blue suit, black turtleneck with a cold, knowing, superior grin.

She turned and saw Vivian. She couldn't return Vivian's encouraging smile. Because if Vivian was there that meant this wasn't a mistake. No, this wasn't a horrible mistake. It was a nightmare come to life.

Corinne swallowed and said in a low, choked voice. "Excuse me one moment please."

She dashed out of the room, into the nearest ladies room, then ran into one of the stalls and locked it.

Deep breaths. She had to take deep breaths. Bursting into tears would be ridiculous and screaming even more so.

She heard the door open and the hurried clicking of high heels.

"Corinne?" Vivian said. "Are you okay?"

No. "I will be in a minute."

"Are you sure?"

"Yes, I just…I'm fine. I didn't expect there to be two other people."

"They're just assistants. He's the only one you need to impress."

Which was the problem. "I'll be right there."

"Everything is going to be okay. You're going to do great."

Corinne briefly closed her eyes, her head suddenly spinning. "Hmm." She heard Vivian walk away and the swinging of the door as it opened and closed.

How could everything be okay? How was she supposed to win *him* over? That was impossible. He probably thought she was mentally unstable. There was no way he'd give his business to her. But she had to try. If he was going to reject her she hoped it would be mercifully quick. He wasn't one to waste time so that might work in her favor.

Corinne left the stall, washed her hands and returned to the conference room. He'd probably indulge her for several minutes and then cut her off and tell her that he'd get back to her. She was fine with that.

"It's a pleasure to have you here Ms. Baylor," the woman to his right said. "You come highly recommended."

Corinne smiled. She wouldn't let Vivian down. "Thank you. The pleasure is all mine."

She saw him slowly blink. Whether from amusement or boredom she couldn't tell. She didn't care. She knew he'd already made up his mind. He wouldn't hire her, he expected her to fail. He already looked disinterested and she hadn't even started. She hadn't even... but she wouldn't be intimidated. No, she wouldn't back down. "Hello, my name is Corinne Baylor from Baylor Events and—"

"Stop."

She stared at him. Did he just tell her to stop? "I'm sorry?"

"I said stop."

He wasn't even going to give her a chance to speak? He didn't even have the decency to give her a chance after she'd come all this way? "If you'll let me—"

He made a dismissive wave of his hand. "Are you allergic to cats?"

"No."

"You're hired." He rested his chin in his hand. "Now that you don't have to try and impress anyone, I want to know what you can do for me."

Hired? Did he say she was hired? Corinne turned to Vivian who just shrugged then motioned for her to continue.

"Well, do you have a particular venue in mind?"

He slowly blinked, displaying that strange disinterested expression again. She assumed that wasn't a good sign.

"Because if you don't," she quickly continued to fill the sudden silence, "I'd suggest the Cameron Mansion. After dwindling business for years they're now under new management and eager for business so I'd easily be able to reserve space for you."

"A mansion? Why not a hotel or a conference center?"

"I think the atmosphere of a mansion will further drive home your message of wealth building. That's the focus of the seminar?" she said, her voice lifting up in a question uncertain if she'd come to the right conclusion.

He blinked. "Is that a question or a statement?"

She cleared her throat. "You're right. First we need to establish what you want to achieve. Do you want a seminar or workshop?"

He paused and she sensed him studying her, but couldn't guess what he saw, she only hoped to look professional instead of terrified. "What are the differences?" he finally said.

It was a sound question and an easy one to answer. "A seminar is primarily lecture based with limited interaction with the audience except for perhaps a question and answer session at the end. However, with a seminar you can have a lot of participants, say one hundred or more. A workshop, on the other hand, is more interactive with a smaller audience size. It allows for a more personalized approach where one or more instructors give demonstrations on a particular topic that participants can try on site."

He rubbed his chin. "Knowing my topic what would you suggest?"

Corinne paused, surprised that he'd ask for her opinion. Vivian had sent her a brief outline prior to their meeting and he seemed to have a lot of ideas. She'd pictured him as the kind of person who would make up his mind and ignore other's advice. "A workshop. You run a large operation but don't have hundreds of employees, plus I feel that participants would learn more from a hands-on approach. Such as having a participatory experience where they calculate the possible return on investment on a made-up venture or participating in an exercise that shows them how to make the most of various assets rather than being lectured to on the importance of them. A workshop would also suit the mansion setting even better.

"Since this will be an aspirational workshop I think getting the attendees in the right mood is essential. They should feel that wealth can be theirs, experience how good it feels to be surrounded by elegance and beautiful things. I believe the location will help them to remember all that you and your speakers will be sharing with them."

He nodded. "I like the workshop idea, but I may not be able to convince some speakers to attend a small workshop. They may be more impressed by a large number."

"If the speaker is more interested in the number of attendees rather than the interest of the participants I'm not sure they're the right speaker for your event. Or rather, the objective of your event. You're not asking them to come for free so they'll be compensated. Also, if there are scheduling issues with someone in another state or country, videoconferencing is an excellent choice so don't limit your options."

He nodded. "Go on."

"I know of an excellent A/V person. I'll review your notes further. I already have an idea that the event should mimic a real financial portfolio—letting people understand how their money can work for them."

"You'll get the final notes by the end of the week." He stood. "There are several things I wish to discuss with you at a later date. Do you have anything planned this time next Tuesday?"

"No."

"Great. I'll contact you with more of the particulars." He shook her hand. "Thank you."

He turned and left. Her palm burned from his touch. But instead of inspiring thoughts of purgatory, the heat he'd inspired reminded her of the heat from a fireplace on a cold night, hot wax drizzled on a bare chest...which was completely inappropriate. Once Brett and his two assistants were gone, Vivian rushed up to her and hugged her.

"You did it! I've never seen him so amenable. Great job."

Corinne absently hugged her back, trying to recover. She couldn't believe the meeting had gone so well. "I don't know what I did."

"Whatever it was, keep it up. I've never seen him like this. I just knew you were the right one for him."

"You mean for the event."

Vivian only smiled.

CHAPTER FIFTEEN

HE WAS WAITING FOR A TRAIN.

Corinne knew she shouldn't have been shocked to see him again at the metro station, but the sight of him standing on the platform still surprised her. She knew she had the advantage since he didn't know she was there, but she wanted to talk to him. She was curious about why he'd chosen her. She'd been certain he didn't like her, especially since he'd seen her at her worse. She swallowed and inched closer to him with all the caution of someone approaching a sleeping, wild animal.

But when she was a foot away she lost her nerve. Did it really matter when the outcome was the same? Obviously he didn't dislike her as much as she'd thought. Or perhaps he pitied her. She could deal with pity. An event like this would be fun to put together. But why had he asked her if she was allergic to cats? Had that made a difference?

Corinne mentally shook her head. It didn't matter.

Everything was settled. She didn't want to ruin this opportunity by asking too many questions. She took a step back no longer eager to talk to him. That's when she noticed he was a man who couldn't seem to stand still. He tapped one foot and then another. But his movements weren't impatient or fidgety. They seemed quick, practiced and efficient. He drummed one hand against his thigh and then the other. He tilted his head to one side and then the other. It was the head exercises that drew her attention to a mark on his neck. A light/dark circular image. She crept closer to get a better look. It looked like a yin and yang tattoo. A tattoo? He had a tattoo? Somehow she wasn't surprised.

He suddenly spun around, his dark gaze meeting hers; she squealed in surprise causing other people to turn towards them. She covered her mouth embarrassed.

"If you want to ask me a question," he said, "do it, otherwise you're invading my space."

That voice, it still grated on her, but he was a client now. And he was now also completely still; nothing about him seemed to move, as if he was focusing all his attention on her like a laser beam.

She lowered her gaze, feeling vulnerable and shy. Why did he have to be so intense? "I'm sorry. I didn't mean to invade your space. I—"

He lifted her chin with his forefinger. "I didn't hear you. Speak up."

His touch left her skin burning. She cleared her throat and raised her voice a little louder, but she kept her gaze lowered. "I said I'm sorry I bothered you."

He bent down and twisted to look up at her like a curious puppy.

She jumped back. "What are you doing?"

He straightened to his full height. "Trying to figure out whether you're talking to me or the floor."

You're an odd man, she wanted to tell him, but held back that thought. He was a client after all.

He bounced up and down on the tips of his toes. "Do you have a question for me or not?"

She lowered her head. "I was just wondering—"

"Speak up."

"I was just wondering—"

He lifted her chin again. "And look at me when you speak."

Her heart pounded. Being this close to him was hard enough, looking at him felt impossible. Why did it matter anyway? She sighed resigned. But if she wanted an answer to her question she had to.

She trembled inside but found the courage to lift her gaze from his shoes and meet his eyes.

Lovely brown eyes in a handsome face that reminded her of the kids who used to tease her, the dates who promised to show up and didn't. A handsome face that had probably been caressed by beautiful women, admired by powerful men. He didn't need to give her a chance, but he had. "Why did you choose me?"

He stopped bouncing. He looked at her for a long moment, so long that she wasn't sure he'd heard her, before he said, "Why wouldn't I choose you?"

"Well, because I—"

"Don't answer that. Never answer a question like that aloud unless you have a counter argument."

She frowned. Was the man talking in riddles? Was he making fun of her? "I don't understand you," she admitted.

"I know," he said with patience. He rested a large hand on her shoulder and gently pushed it back, causing her to stand straighter. "That's why I'm trying to explain it to you." He rested his hands on his hips and although his gaze never left her face she got the impression he was studying her—again. She wished she knew what he saw. "You have to sell yourself. When I ask, 'Why wouldn't I choose you?' I mean why would an intelligent man like me be stupid enough to *not* choose you?"

Her frown deepened. This man was definitely strange, but intriguing. She'd never thought of it that way. Never thought that choosing her would be the rational decision.

"You're saying that I was the most rational choice?"

"I'm saying that's the way you should see it."

"Oh." She lowered her gaze. "But that still doesn't answer my question."

He bent and looked up at her again.

She stepped back surprised he could twist his body so easily. "Stop doing that."

"Then stop talking to the floor. I'm starting to get jealous. I'm the one who hired you after all."

She threw up her hands exasperated and stared at him. "Exactly! Why?"

He scratched his cheek. "Why?"

"Yes, why?"

He shrugged. "I don't know. Maybe because you came highly recommended, you have an impressive history, your ideas are sound."

"But you didn't hear my ideas until after you hired me. Is it because of the cats?"

"Cats?"

"You asked about cats. Whether I was allergic."

"Oh, right. No, I only asked because I was curious."

"Then why?"

He folded his arms and slowly blinked.

She was starting to sense that meant something but she wasn't sure what. "You looked terrified," he said. "Scared. You left the room as if you wanted to hide."

The train arrived and opened its doors. He stepped inside and turned to her. Although the train was also hers, she was scared to get on.

She felt her cheeks burn. It had been that obvious? She couldn't ride with him. She'd wait for the next one. People pushed past her to get on.

"So you felt sorry for me?" she said.

"No, I admired you."

A warning sound that the doors would soon close echoed in the station.

"Why?"

"Because you came back." He winked. "That's when I knew you were the one for me."

The doors closed.

CHAPTER SIXTEEN

You were the one for me.

He hadn't meant to say it like that, but it was true.

"You're grinning. Why are you grinning?"

Brett groaned as he walked past the well-dressed black woman with straight chin length, highlighted brown hair, standing on his doorstep. He'd thanked the driver who'd driven him home from the metro station and had hoped to come home to peace. "What are you doing here?"

She pursed her lips. "Is that anyway to greet your mother?"

He opened the door then motioned her forward. "Do I have to greet her at all?"

"That's better, rudeness suits you. You're still not driving?"

"I drive sometimes," he said, which wasn't a complete lie. "What are you doing here?"

"What were you grinning about? You looked ridiculous."

He hadn't realized he was grinning, but talking to Corinne had put him in a good mood.

Corinne amused him. She was so eager to please, usually people like that annoyed him. He'd been prepared to be annoyed—after he'd gotten over his shock—when she'd first entered the conference room.

He couldn't deny that he'd noticed her lattice patterned stockings and the glitter of gold in her ear. When she'd bumped into him and dropped her portfolio in the station, he'd felt sorry for the harried looking woman. She looked so nervous, but determined, and something about her made him wonder why she seemed so familiar. It was only when their eyes met and her expression changed that he realized she'd been *that* woman.

That woman who'd looked so distraught only a week ago that she'd stepped close to the edge of the platform. He hoped that if he hadn't been there she wouldn't have done anything. But then seeing her again, she looked nothing like that woman. That other woman had hollow eyes, sunken cheeks, like she hadn't eaten in days. Her hair was dull, pulled back in a messy puff.

But this woman. This woman was pretty with a rosier complexion and sharp brown eyes. At first, he wasn't sure she was the same woman. But the startled recognition on her face confirmed it.

He never suspected she'd be the event planner Vivian had recommended. When she stepped into the conference room, froze like a scared animal and then dashed out of the room, Brett was prepared for her to come up with an excuse to leave. It wouldn't be the first time to have someone come up with an emergency to avoid having to face him.

But then she'd come back. Terrified. His heart swelled with admiration when she'd returned, it was an emotion he rarely felt anymore. He hadn't lied to her. That was the moment he knew she was someone he wanted to know. Someone he was eager to see again.

"You're doing it again," his mother said.

"What?"

"Grinning. It's not like you. Are you on some sort of medication or something?"

Brett closed the front door and set his keys in the ceramic bowl resting on a small table in the foyer before he bent down and pet Martha and Alvin his two long haired calico cats. "What do you want?"

Martha quickly darted out of the way to avoid having her tail crushed under his mother's black high heels. His mother marched to his kitchen and took a seat. "You need to do something about your father."

"Encourage him to seek a divorce?"

She narrowed her eyes. "That's not funny."

He pulled down a pouch of treats from the cupboard and handed each cat one in sympathy for having to endure their unwanted guest.

He wasn't trying to be funny. His mother always had some criticism about his father that she wanted Brett to help her with. How his parents had stayed married as long as they had was still a mystery to him. He put the treat pouch away and washed his hands before he poured two glasses of grape juice then handed her one. "What is it now?"

She took a quick sip then set the glass down. "He's bored. Restless. He doesn't know what to do with himself."

He took a seat in front of her and shrugged. "So?"

"Retirement doesn't suit him. Give him a job," she said, instructing him as if he were one of the dental assistants she used to work with in her practice.

Brett shook his head. "I'm not sure that's a good idea."

"It's an excellent idea."

"Because you thought of it?"

"No, because it would solve the problem."

"What if he says 'no'?"

"He won't say 'no'. I'll make sure of it. Just give him something that will last a minimum of three hours a day. That shouldn't be hard."

Brett drummed his fingers against the side of the glass. "I'll see what I can do. Is that all?"

"Are you going to tell me why you were grinning?"

"No."

"You can call him tomorrow."

Brett sighed. "I have to come up with an idea first. I can't call and say 'Hey Dad, I have an imaginary job for you.'"

"I know coming up with a job won't take you long. You're always full of ideas. I'll be waiting."

"Yes. Of course." He stood and gently took her arm, lifting her to her feet. "I have some work to do." He escorted her to the front door.

"Have you bought another property?"

He opened the door. "Bye Mom."

"Started another business?"

"I'll call you soon."

"Why were you grinning?"

"Drive safe."

"Is it a woman?"

He flashed her an indulgent grin before he closed the door. He loved his mother but she was one to sour a good mood. She was right, he could easily find something for his father to do. How long he could keep him busy was something else entirely. He took out his cell phone and noticed a text from Vivian.

Thanks. You won't regret this.

I know.

He thought of Corinne's face as the metro doors closed. This time instead of grinning, he smiled.

"Does he have tattoos?"

That hadn't been the first question Corinne had expected to ask Vivian when she called her later that evening, but it had been swirling in her mind. She told herself it was because she wanted to know more about her client, but she knew that was a lie.

I knew you were the one for me.

She wasn't sure if it was the wink, the way he looked at her, or his words, but when the train pulled from the station she felt like she could burst into flames. Everything about him was so strange, yet sensuous. The way he moved, the shape of his mouth, the way his gaze swept over her face.

"Hello, to you too," Vivian said with a laugh.

Corinne sat on her sofa and tucked her feet underneath her. "I'm sorry."

"Who doesn't have tattoos nowadays?"

"We don't."

"Besides us."

"And I know Bonnie and her husband Greg don't so statistically—"

"Never mind," Vivian said with a groan. "I'm sorry I said anything. Why do you ask?"

"I'm just curious."

"You're not the only one. There are rumors he has seven."

"Seven?"

"I don't know how the rumor started but people have been guessing. One woman says she's noticed three. I guess the rest are in places one can't easily see. Why do you ask?"

"I thought I saw one on his neck."

"That yin and yang symbol, right?"

"Yes, that's the one."

"Uh-huh," Vivian said. "I asked him about it once."

"And?"

"Like I said, I asked him about it *once*. He gave me *that* look, changed the subject and I never talked about it again."

Corinne furrowed her brows. "That look?"

"You haven't seen it yet. No, of course you wouldn't have, but you will and you won't forget it. You feel like you've just been stung by a scorpion. But as long as you don't try to pry into his private life you should be fine."

"Right."

Vivian hesitated. "Don't be fooled. He's easier to work with than some of the nightmare clients you have—"

"Hey!"

"But he's not as easygoing as he seemed today."

"I don't think he's easygoing at all."

"Good," Vivian said relieved. "After your meeting with him went so well, I briefly thought you might have a better chance with him than anyone else, but then I changed my mind. People underestimate him, he's generous but he's also guarded. He has a past that he really doesn't like to talk about. I respect that. He's the kind of man who sets up boundaries you don't try to cross. You know the conference room where we met is one of the business properties his company manages. He usually uses different locations so people don't see where he really works."

"You mean that's not the Quest headquarters?"

"It's the place he takes people to who need to be impressed, but if you get a chance, you'll eventually see where he *really* works. Even then, don't be fooled that he's letting you get close."

"You don't have to worry about me, Vivian. A man who takes pictures while hidden in the shadows is not someone I expect to get close to."

But that night she did. In her dream. She and Brett were intimately close.

It was the same dream as before with the train

turning into a dragon, but this time she didn't ride the dragon alone. Brett rode behind her. She felt his muscular thighs against hers, his solid arms wrapped around her waist, her back pressed against his chest. But instead of feeling shy she felt powerful as she held the reins of the dragon and they sailed through the sky. She felt his lips against her neck as he slowly branded her with kisses. His breath felt hot against her skin when he said, "You are the one for me."

"The only one?" she said.

"There could never be anyone else. Take me wherever you want to go."

She smiled. "You trust me?"

"Always."

And the dragon soared higher taking them above the clouds and then it fell away and she thought she was falling until she realized she wasn't. She was lying naked in a bed of clouds and Brett lay beside her and she felt his body come close and...

The sound of her alarm woke her from her thoughts. She pushed the sheets away sweaty and embarrassed. What had come over her? He'd complimented her; was that enough to dream of him that way? Hadn't Vivian warned her that he wasn't a man to even think of as a romantic prospect?

This was business.

Solely business.

She couldn't expect anything more.

CHAPTER SEVENTEEN

BUT SHE DID.

She couldn't seem to help herself.

She'd started making up reasons to see him, which didn't help because then her dreams of him became even more vivid, but she couldn't seem to stop. It had been nearly a month since their first official meeting and he'd become like a drug to her. A drug that both aggravated and thrilled her.

Most times she tried to control her emotions and be professional.

Most times they would text, email, video chat, but then—somehow—she would come up with a reason to see him in person and to her surprise Brett never turned her down. She wondered about that. And she wondered about herself. Why did he intrigue her so much? He wasn't her type at all. He had her thinking about tattoos and naughty dance moves. Nothing like Harrison or any other man she'd been with. Plus he was a client. She never dated clients, however once the event was over...

But their second meeting had been the beginning of her downfall. The second time she met him they had been alone in the conference room—no assistants, no Vivian—and at first she was worried that their interaction would be stilted. Instead their conversation went smoothly and she found that when she was talking about work, looking at him was vastly easier. Too easy. He looked at her with an interested eagerness that she couldn't get enough of. She knew what she was doing and he needed her help so it made her feel like an equal. He asked for her ideas and listened.

Really listened. It was so...arousing. She never knew having an intelligent, handsome man listen to her every word with genuine interest could be so stimulating.

But it was still just business. Nothing more could come of it. It would never work on a more personal level. He probably already had someone and she wanted to focus on her business. She had to.

But she liked how he challenged her. How he made her see things in a new way. How he made her see herself. He wasn't a nightmare. He was one of the easiest men to work with. When she'd attended one of their meetings exhausted, she'd told him about Phyllis' function, which amazingly she'd saved from being the complete disaster she'd feared. He slowly blinked said "Then let this be the last time," before he changed the subject.

But she couldn't. He didn't understand, just like Vivian.

"She isn't—"

"When you have a choice why would you choose the worst option?"

"I need the work."

"You'll work twice as hard with the wrong clients. You need to value your services more."

Vivian had said the same thing, she knew he was right. But she was scared, but he didn't need to know that. She twirled a pen between her fingers, careful to remind herself not to stick it in her hair, and glanced down at her notes. "I forgot to ask. Since you're offering a lot of information would you consider, perhaps, paring down some of it?"

"No."

Her head shot up at the finality of his tone. "But you're giving a lot of information away for free." She couldn't believe the extent of financial information he was including in the workshop. She knew she'd have to schedule enough time to make copies of everything and get all the material compiled.

He shrugged. "So? I want my employees to enjoy wealth as much as I do."

"But—"

"I like the idea of the mansion, the design of the workshop binder for each attendee," he said, referring to the faux leather, zipped portfolio binders with convenient pockets for cell phones, tablets, pens, business cards, handout materials and a clipboard with a large writing notepad. "They are all suitable."

"It's a very generous idea, but people rarely appreciate things given to them for free."

"Maybe not right away but they'll thank me."

Corinne sighed, resigned. "Then I'll make sure they have a day they never forget."

"That's what I expect."

Never settle for less. The words from the oath came to her. He was the kind of man who lived it. The oath now had a new meaning to her. Was this what they meant? Had she been settling for terrible clients?

The next time she got an opportunity to refuse a project, she knew it would be hard but she looked at the prospect and said, "I'm not the right event planner for you. I'm sorry," and she briefly felt ill and imagined her calendar of events becoming blank, which would be a true nightmare, but then the feeling left. She felt relieved. Working with Brett had spoiled her. She didn't want to work with clients who belittled her or changed their minds at the last minute anymore. He was right. She had to value what she did.

But her business hadn't been the only change over the past several weeks. She'd had a brief talk with Jason to find out how he was doing. "Okay" was the most he would reveal. Her first scheduled weekend visit with him, she'd taken him to the movies, hadn't revealed much more about how he was doing in school, or what he was learning. But she hoped to slowly get close to him again.

However, right now she was getting ready to see Brett again for the—fourth? Fifth?—time but this time in his main office, the one Vivian had mentioned was the place where he really worked. The place she'd never been before since they'd always met downtown in the conference room.

This time, instead of a high rise building in the heart of the city, she'd driven to a cozy little community that rested on the line of the Maryland/DC divide and parked in front of a four-story glass structure.

He'd invited her there because she'd managed to come up with the flimsy excuse that he needed to see the mockup for the handouts in person to make sure the quality of the paper she had selected was up to his standards.

She was certain he was going to see through her ruse this time, but, as always, he'd quickly agreed to see her. She couldn't believe how many times they'd met for a one day event. She'd never worked this closely with a client before and in several weeks it would be over. She didn't want to think about that.

She sat outside his office, located on the top floor, in the waiting area next to a balding, chubby black man who looked nervous. But what had first caught her attention wasn't his expression, but the sound of his knitting needles as he expertly knit green baby booties. She glanced at the large canvas bag next to his foot and also noticed more yarn, a scarf, another pair of baby booties and what looked like a baby blanket. He was clearly prolific in his hobby. She knew some people used knitting as stress relief. She wondered what had him stressed now. Was he there to sell his services? Ask for a job? He looked so unsettled she felt a little sorry for him.

She nodded to the bootie and said to him, "That's lovely. Someone's going to be very lucky to get that."

He smiled. "Thanks."

"Are you here to see Mr. Lattimore?"

He nodded. His brown eyes wide and vulnerable behind his silver framed glasses. "I'm here for a job."

"Me too," she said, trying to hide her surprise. He looked to be around seventy-something and as awkward as a kid interviewing for their first job.

His brows shot up. "You're here for a job too?"

"Yes, no. I mean I have a job, but I'm working with him."

"Y-you know him?"

"A little."

"Is he as scary as they say?"

"Scary?"

The man lowered his voice. "I heard that he's got tattoos covering his body. That he was once part of a gang and that's how he's gotten some of the properties he manages. Through intimidation."

Corinne allowed the image of Brett's bare body covered in tattoos to flash through her mind before she brushed it away. "From what I've read about him that's complete malarkey."

"You've read about him?" he asked and Corinne smiled, impressed that he could hold a conversation while his needles continued to click away in a rhythmic motion.

"Sure. He's been featured in a number of top publications."

"You seem very impressed by him."

"Oh, I am. I admire him a lot. Not only what he's achieved but by what he does for others."

"I don't even know what he looks like. My wife forced me to come here."

"I won't lie. His looks can be...intimidating. But

he's sharp."

The older man smiled. "For a woman who says she knows a little, you seem to know a lot about him."

"No, I'm able to read people well. It helps me to work with them better. He's generous and caring, but hides it so that he doesn't get taken advantage of." She tapped the side of her nose before she pointed at him. "But knowing that secret then the advantage can be yours."

The sound of the knitting needles paused briefly before starting again. "Married?"

"Him or me?"

He shrugged.

Corinne didn't take offense to his question. One generation's nosiness was another generation's innocent curiosity.

"Well, I'm not anymore. I don't know anything about his personal life. It's none of my business if he's married or seeing someone. Although I'm dying to know." She bit her lip, shocked by her candor. "I mean...because it would give me a fuller picture of him a-as a person." She released a nervous little laugh. "But he's great to work with so you have nothing to worry about."

"That's good to know Ms.—"

"Oh, I'm sorry." She held out her hand. "Corinne Baylor. I'm an event planner. I'm helping Mr. Lattimore with an upcoming workshop. His employees are lucky to have him and I'm sure you'll enjoy working with him or anyone in the company."

The man nodded. He set his knitting aside, letting his smile broaden. "I know I will now," he said and suddenly he looked like a savvy gentleman and no longer like a scared elderly man. But before she could react, the office door opened and Brett stepped out and said, "What are you doing here?"

Corinne rose to her feet startled. "I thought we had an appointment."

"Of course we do," Brett said softening his tone. "I'm talking to him."

She rushed forward and said in a low voice, "Be nice. He's a little nervous."

Brett sighed. "Dad, what have you been telling her?"

She turned to the other man stunned. "Dad?" They looked nothing alike. Like a bear claiming a giraffe as its offspring.

"Nothing," the older man said, rising to his feet. "And why shouldn't I be here? I'm only an hour early."

"You were supposed to come tomorrow," Brett said.

His father shoved his hands in his pockets. "Well, the journey was worth it. I got to meet your delightful event planner." He rocked on his heels. "And just what kind of event are you two planning, hmm?"

His eyes danced with amusement. He made their relationship sound more intimate than it was. She couldn't believe how easily he'd been able to trick her and how she'd gushed about his son. He was probably used to it.

"Go home, Dad."

"You're sure I can't help?"

"I'm sure."

He grinned at Corinne. "That personal thing you were wondering about?" he said, reminding her of their conversation about Brett's marital status. "He's not."

CHAPTER EIGHTEEN

"Sorry about that," Brett said in a tone she'd never heard before. He didn't seem the type who was easily embarrassed, but something about seeing his father had bothered him.

Not as sorry as I am, she wanted to say, her cheeks burning. How could she have been so open about her curiosity about whether Brett was single or not? What if his father told him what she'd said? What if...?

Brett snapped his fingers in front of her face. "Are you okay?"

"Yes, yes. Sorry."

He closed the door and motioned to one of the plush seats. For a moment she didn't move. His office was nothing like she'd expected. Aside from the size, it was a lot larger than she would have guessed, and the desk, which reminded her it was a room used for work, it was designed like an elegant lounge with two bold, colorful abstract paintings hanging on the wood paneled walls, a large potted plant in the corner, a stylish couch and two muted colored, red armchairs. It was a shocking departure from the cool greys, browns and blues of the conference room where she was used to seeing him. This setting seemed more intimate and personal. As if she were seeing another side to him. A man who took pleasure in surprise, aesthetics and design.

He wore the same ice blue suit that he had at their first meeting. But this time she didn't see a cold unfeeling man who inspired thoughts of glaciers and icecaps. Instead she thought of starlight and cloudless blue skies, things both wondrous and out of reach.

"Take a seat," he said, "but mind the cats."

She stared at him not ready to sit down yet. "You have cats?"

He held up two fingers.

"Two?"

He nodded.

"I dreamt that you had two pets."

He blinked. "You dreamt about me?"

Corinne froze, realizing her mistake. Again?! What was wrong with her today? "No, no of course not. Why would I dream about you?" she said with a laugh. She opened her portfolio and pulled out some papers as an excuse not to look at him. "What I meant was I *thought* about you having pets because..." She searched her mind for a reason, setting the papers on the armrest on the nearest chair. "Because you asked if I was allergic to cats."

"Okay."

She looked around the room and scanned the ground

to make sure she wouldn't step on the cats, but they seemed to be hiding. "What are their names?"

"Martha and Alvin. I have to take one to the vet later and they like coming with me here so..."

She carefully sat down then felt something furry brush against her leg. Before she could look down to see what it was, she heard something land on the wide armrest beside her. She turned and saw two yellowish-green eyes sniffing the air before the cat sat and stared at her. The way the cat studied her reminded her of its owner, she couldn't guess what it was thinking. Did it want to play? Jump on her? Be petted?

"Sorry about that," Brett said not sounding very apologetic, "Alvin's always curious."

Corinne held out her hand slowly, not wanting to frighten the animal with any sudden moves, so that the cat could smell it. Once he did, the cat seemed satisfied, curled up into a ball and closed its eyes.

"Did you train him to do that?"

Brett sat in a seat facing her. "To sleep? No cats do that on their own."

She opened her mouth to clarify then decided against it. He really could be aggravating sometimes. She crossed her legs. "Where's the other one?"

"Somewhere hiding. Martha's more shy."

"I'd say she was more polite." She looked at the sleeping cat, "You're sleeping on my papers you know." The indolent cat opened one eye with feline disinterest before it closed it again. She tried to slide the papers out from under it with little success.

Brett snapped his fingers and the cat's ears twitched. "Come."

The cat made a disgruntled sound before it stretched its front legs; open its mouth in a wide yawn then stepped down and walked across Corinne's lap before it jumped to the floor. Alvin sauntered over to Brett and brushed against his leg before disappearing under the desk.

Brett turned his attention to her and said, "Shall we start?"

"Yes," she said impressed he had managed to train the cat somehow.

She handed him the mockups. "There are two types. Tell me which one you prefer."

He looked down at the paper choices, placed one on his lap and ran his hand over the front of the other before rubbing the corner between his forefinger and thumb to assess the weight. He did the same with the other paper. "Are you always this attentive to detail?" He lifted his gaze to capture hers. "Or is it just me?"

She'd been caught. He knew. He *knew*. But he couldn't know. This had to be business. Professional only. At least until the event was over. "No. I try to make sure that every client is happy with the event I help organize for them."

He studied her for a moment and she waited to see if he'd let her lie slide. He nodded. "Okay." He handed her the lighter weighted sample. "I like this one."

"Great." She took the papers from him and quickly shoved them in her portfolio. She'd wasted enough of his time and her own. It was time to stop acting on her school girl crush. It would be even worse if his father said anything...No she wouldn't think about that. The next time she saw Brett would be at the workshop then she'd disappear from his life. "Then that's everything. Leave the rest to me."

"That's it?"

Did he think she'd wasted his time? "Well, yes, I realize you're a busy man but I thought it was important that you saw the quality of the paper first hand instead of—"

"What are you doing after this?"

"Uh... I will be meeting with the manager at the Cameron Mansion to finalize details."

"Great." He stood. "I'll join you."

She was supposed to be creating distance not taking him along. "No, you can't."

He paused. "Why not?"

"Because...because I sent you a link so that you can take a 3D tour of the mansion online when you have a chance. It's like you're practically there."

"But it's not the same as actually being there, is it? A 3D visual does not give me the sights, smells and sounds that I need to really understand what a place is about. How my employees will experience it. I want to see what it's like firsthand. We'll take your car since you know where the mansion is." Brett pulled out his cell phone and then said to the person on the other side, "I'm going out for no more than two hours. Alvin and Martha are in my office. You know what to do. Yes. Yes. Thanks." He put the phone away. "Okay, let's go."

CHAPTER NINETEEN

He belonged there.

Corinne watched Brett as he walked underneath the large chandelier in one of the expansive ballroom inside the Cameron Mansion with the manager, the manager's assistant close at hand, to answer any question as they provided a private tour.

But while Corinne found the surroundings spectacular, from the crystal vases to the vast expanse of windows, her gaze never strayed far from him. Brett had not been carefully crafted by human hands like the objects in the mansion, but there was still a remarkable beauty about him. About how he walked, spoke; as if he were always in command even when it didn't seem like he needed to be. He had presence. She couldn't understand why a man who was so fascinating to look at would choose to take pictures that hid him in the shadows.

She continued to be completely intrigued and transfixed by the way he moved. Sometimes she even tried to imitate the tilt of his chin and found herself walking straighter; she would modulate her gait and find that she'd become more sure-footed. It was like he had a secret to movement she'd never been taught. Then a thought came to her mind and she finally understood what had captured her. The way he moved wasn't ordinary. It wasn't accidental. He moved... "Like a dancer. Were you a dancer?"

It was only when Brett stopped walking halfway across the ballroom that she realized she'd posed her question aloud without meaning to, cutting into the manager's eloquently verbose speech about the mansion's amenities.

Brett slowly spun around, it felt like an eternity, and for a moment Corinne could picture him on a stage commanding an audience with that one powerful move.

"Excuse me?"

She waved her hands. "Nothing. It was nothing." She nodded to the manager. "I'm sorry, please continue."

The manager sent Brett a nervous glance then hesitantly did so. Brett kept his gaze on her for a long, painful moment before he turned back around and continued walking. Corinne grabbed the front of her blouse and reminded herself to breathe.

This was why she had to stay away from him. Vivian had warned her. He wasn't someone she could get close to. He had a past. He had boundaries one didn't cross lightly.

Even if she'd been curious she should have asked him privately not in front of others. Not that there was anything wrong with dancing...

She set the idea aside and listened to the rest of the tour hoping Brett would agree that the mansion was an ideal location and not change his mind like some of her other clients did.

To her relief he didn't say anything as they walked back to her car. She tried to hurry, but he set the pace, walking with a slow, steadied gait. She didn't care. She'd survived their final meeting. She'd drop him back at his office. Take a cold shower...

"I heard what you said," he said in a low voice that seemed to be carried along by the warm April breeze, sending goosebumps skittering along her skin.

"What?"

"In the mansion. I heard what you said. I want to know why you said it."

She feigned innocence. "I said a lot of things. I don't know—"

"About dance."

She sighed defeated. She was caught. She might as well admit it. "I just...wondered if you were a dancer."

"Why?"

"I think dancers are—"

He slowly blinked and repeated his question with more force. "Why?"

She bit her lip. He was upset and that was the last thing she wanted. "I asked if you danced because I like the way..." She let her words trail off. She couldn't say "I like the way you move", that would be inappropriate. "You move so beautifully," she finished feeling ridiculous. She shouldn't be watching him that closely anyway. She unlocked her car with the press of her key fob. "I'm sorry, never mind."

He blinked. "Yes." He got into the passenger's side and closed the door.

Yes? Yes, what? Yes, that he used to dance? or Yes, that they should forget she even asked? She bit her lip and got into the driver's seat.

She stole glances at him on their quiet ride back. He was more composed than usual. Usually he was constantly in motion. Drumming his fingers against his thigh, moving his shoulders, shifting his foot, but now he sat still—stock still—and stared out the window with a fixed expression. Like a wooden statue. Since she'd already come this far she might as well hazard a guess. "Tap, jazz, street dance, ballet?"

He sent her a long look, it wasn't the scorpion stare Vivian had warned her about, but it had the similar warning as the shake of a rattlesnake's tail that said *Stay Away*, before he returned his gaze to the road ahead of them.

She got the message. It had to be the later 'yes', the 'yes' that meant he wanted her to forget she'd mentioned dancing. His past was off-limits.

"Just for the record, I think dancers are amazing. The discipline and skill; how they push their bodies to the limit."

"I'm not a dancer," he said. But somehow she also heard 'anymore' and that intrigued her more than if he hadn't said anything at all, but she knew this was as far as she'd get with him. It wasn't her place. He was only a client and soon he wouldn't be. He'd been a nice fantasy.

That's all her life had been right now. The society had been fun, but it had hardly brought a new man in her life. But after the Quest workshop she hoped she'd get a few good referrals from him.

Brett pulled out his cell phone and began to quickly type something.

"I'm sorry," she finally said.

He rested the phone down. "Don't be."

But she was. She'd broken some fragile bond that they'd had. She'd ruined something good. She pulled in front of his building and parked. "Right. Well...see you next month."

He looked at her surprised. "Next month?"

"At the workshop."

He blinked once, then twice before he said, "We don't need to meet for any...reason?"

"No, this is it. My schedule's gotten busier and I'm sure yours has too."

He sent her one of his long, considering looks before he nodded and said, "Okay."

"Right. Bye." She waved and drove away, wishing she could leave her feelings of attraction behind just as easily as she could him.

CHAPTER TWENTY

SHE'D GUESSED.

How could she have guessed?

Instead of taking the elevator Brett walked up the stairs to his office welcoming the exercise. His body hummed with...damn what was this strange new sensation? Fear? Dread? Shock?

How could she have guessed?!! He'd been very careful in how he separated his past from his present life. He'd lived the life of a civilian, which was how dancers thought of non-dancers.

But somehow she'd seen who he used to be and that terrified him. He'd buried that man years ago. Covered him up with all his dark regrets and secrets and forced himself to forget. He'd changed. He wasn't that man anymore. He'd created a new image. There was nothing of the passionate, adventurer he used to be. Now his life was about stability, investment, planning for the future.

For nearly a decade his past had been his shadow

realm, a place only few people knew about, a place he rarely visited. He'd grown comfortable with the split he'd devised, but Corinne, with one statement, had shoved his two worlds together threatening an explosion.

It was her lack of surprise that troubled him the most. She spoke as if being a dancer and business owner were completely compatible. As if she were sewing up two halves of a man and making him whole. But he wasn't whole. He knew that more than anyone. She certainly couldn't know that. But she'd guessed anyway.

That made him feel exposed, vulnerable. He hated that. He wondered if she hated that too. If that was why she hadn't come up with another reason to see him again. If she'd realized he wasn't the man she'd thought he was. It had been a risk to show her his office and the cats. Had he unknowingly revealed hints of his past...?

He reached the fourth floor, turned down the hall and headed towards his office.

He'd miss her, but it was best they parted ways now before he grew too attached. She'd amused him. He'd found her comfortable and refreshing in a world of pretense. But getting attached was dangerous.

"I like her."

Brett jumped and spun around at the sound of his father's voice.

His father laughed. "I haven't been able to startle you like that since you were a kid."

He scowled, feeling his face burn with both embarrassment and resentment. "What are you still doing here?"

"I have nowhere else to go."

That was a lie, but he let it pass. He'd managed to come up with a way to put his father's favorite hobby—knitting—to good use. He now knitted baby booties, caps and blankets for preemies and newborns for two area hospitals and scarves and gloves for a local homeless shelter. Crafting and delivering his creations kept his father busy enough to keep his mother happy, but Brett still invited his father to lunch every now and then just to make sure. Brett headed to his office.

His father followed. "Did you hear what I said?"

"No."

"I like her."

"I'm glad for you. She seemed to like you too."

"That's interesting."

Brett opened his office door and walked inside. "What is?"

"That you knew to whom I was referring."

Brett smirked, remembering his father had been a professor of etymology, a branch of linguistic studies focused on the origin of words. "Is thou sure I knew to whom thou so referred?" he teased him.

His father frowned. "Whom is a real word."

"Used last century. Few use it that way anymore."

"I don't care." His father sat and placed his large canvas bag on the ground. Martha jumped up to his side in greeting. "She likes you in case you were wondering."

All the time. "I wasn't."

"You should have heard the glowing praise she was heaping on you this morning. Have you asked her out yet?"

"We're working together."

"She's not an employee, therefore, I very much doubt that would be a problem. However, did you know that the word 'employee' originated from—"

"I'm not interested."

"In her or my explanation?"

"Take a guess." Brett sat behind his desk. Perhaps, despite his knitting projects, his father still had too much time on his hands. But he'd have to endure his father's lack of more to do. Brett knew he either had to hear his mother complaining about his father being underfoot or he'd have to deal with his father teasing him. He'd take the teasing.

"Your mother told me you were grinning about something the other day."

"That was weeks ago. Don't you two have better things to talk about?"

"Unfortunately, no." His father paused before he said, "She seems to have a strong personality. Very amiable and forthcoming."

Brett sniffed, wondering how his father had formed that opinion. "She's easily terrified. Trust me."

"That doesn't mean she's not worth the risk. People gain courage in the strangest ways."

"You don't know that."

His father's gaze sharpened. "So you are interested?"

He'd revealed too much. "Right now I have to focus on work."

"That's all you've focused on."

"I've dated—"

"Women who will never threaten your heart."

He sighed. "Do we really need to do this now?"

"You know of a better time?"

"Sure. Never fits on my schedule, how about yours?"

"So you're fine pouring your heart into your cats and trying to improve the lives of your employees? While that's admirable you still end up alone."

"I'm not alone."

"Ghosts don't count."

Brett gripped his hand into a fist. His father knew him too well. Knew too much about him. Could strip him bare and see all his scars and flaws; see wounds so blistered and deep that he felt like an ugly man. Beautiful? Corinne had said he moved so beautifully. Why had he let that seep in? Why had it touched him? He shouldn't have let those words even come close to his heart. But the soft, awkward way she'd said them had surprised him. He wanted to know more. He knew she was eager to listen if he told her. Most people were curious about him. He was an oddity. Always had been. It had never bothered him before. The different personas he made for himself worked and protected him. Only this last persona had become something of a prison. Something of a tomb. His father knew it, he knew it, but he wasn't ready to change.

"I'm worried about your mother, though," his father said with a tired sigh.

Brett stiffened. "Why? What's wrong?"

"I'm not sure Ms. Baylor could handle your mother."

Brett groaned. "Dad, it's not going to happen. I'm not dating Corinne."

"Did she like the cats?"

"I don't know. Doesn't matter."

"Then why use them as a test?"

"I didn't use them—" He stopped when his father gave him a knowing look. "Alvin needs to go to the vet—"

His father shook his head. "He went last week."

Brett stared at him.

His father stared back.

He swore and surrendered. "Fine. So I was curious how she would react."

"And?"

"Alvin fell asleep on her papers."

"And how did she respond?"

Brett remembered the look on her face with affection. She looked adorable and tried to figure out what to do next. She wasn't sure if she should pick Alvin up, push him aside or poke him. "I rescued her."

His father's eyes shone bright. "You're grinning again."

He covered his mouth and forced his grin to drop. "So what?"

"You haven't grinned like that in a long time. It's not every day you meet someone who's good for you."

"You're making too much out of this. I was only curious, it's not—"

"Ask her out. You're not one to let an opportunity slip through your fingers."

He knew that she liked him. He'd never had anyone be as attentive to him as she had been these last several weeks. She still hesitated to look directly at him when they weren't talking about work, but she was gaining confidence and he liked that. He liked a lot about her. He liked how she sometimes mimicked his movements—the way she would stand or sit forward in her chair. He didn't know why, but he found it endearing.

He'd known she was making up reasons to see him and he'd followed her lead because he was having fun and he knew it would end. It had to end. A woman like her couldn't handle a man like him. He wouldn't want her to. He'd tried that once. He'd never get that close again. He couldn't trust her to be strong. He knew how fragile she really was in spite of the new clothes and her slowly rising confidence.

He'd never forget the woman who'd walked towards the edge of the platform...

He felt the weight of a man's grip on his shoulder. He'd been so lost in his thoughts that he hadn't noticed his father had moved to stand behind him. He closed his eyes. "Don't."

His father's grip tightened. It didn't hurt but he wished it did. "Pretending you don't care won't change the fact that you do."

"Dad—"

He spun Brett's chair around, forcing him to face him, his voice as determined as his gaze. "Listen to me. I can't stand to see another year go by with you living in the past. I don't care about how many futures you help to make better, how many dreams you help to come true when you sacrifice yourself in the process. You're too young to start dying now. She may not be the one. It may not work out, but what she said about you—"

Brett looked away, annoyed by how the thought of Corinne gave him hope, shook his heart. "She doesn't know me. Not really."

His father tapped Brett's cheek. "Look at me. A Lattimore doesn't look away."

Brett took a deep breath and shifted his gaze. He saw the love in his father's eyes and the worry and it tore him apart. "I'm sorry."

"You don't have to apologize anymore. You can move on. All the things she said about you were true. They weren't empty words of flattery. She didn't know who I was so she had no need to impress me. She spoke about you with pure admiration."

"But she doesn't know—"

"I don't think it will make a difference. But you won't know if you don't have the courage to try." He patted him on the shoulder. "Come on, let's get a drink." He grinned. "Your treat."

CHAPTER TWENTY-ONE

CORINNE WAS NEARLY HOME when she realized Brett had forgotten his cell phone. Just her luck. All the other times she'd had to make up excuses to see him and now she had a legitimate one and she dreaded it. Clearly she'd upset him more than he'd let on if he'd left his phone behind.

She returned to his building and was stepping out of the elevator when she saw one of his assistants racing down the hall. Her name was Alyssa and Corinne had always found the young black woman with gold conch shell earrings and light brown eyes to be friendly and courteous. Today she looked frightened.

She stopped in front of Corinne and stared at her wide eyed. "Did you see anything?"

"What do you expect me to see?"

"Everyone's gone and I'm the only one here. You've got to help me before Brett gets back."

"Help you with what?"

She grabbed Corinne's arm and dragged her towards Brett's office. "He went out with his father and asked me to look after them."

"The cats?" Corinne guessed.

Alyssa nodded before she pulled Corinne into Brett's office and closed the door.

"Okay, but why do you need my help?"

"He asked me to put them in their carriers so that he could just pick them up when he gets back."

"And?"

"Martha's missing. I didn't lock the carrier the way I should have. What should I do?"

"Look for her."

"I've looked everywhere," she said with a note of desperation.

"Well, at least you kept the office door closed so she couldn't have…" Her words faded when she saw the look of chagrin on Alyssa's face. "You didn't."

"I left the office door open for a couple minutes, that's all. I thought it would be okay since they were locked up."

"Well, she's somewhere on this floor because the exit to the stairwell is closed and the doors to the elevator closes fast. Someone would have noticed a cat climbing on. That's something."

"Brett'll be coming back soon and—"

"Okay, you check the other places and I'll check the waiting room and his office again."

They split up and for the next several minutes frantically searched for the missing cat.

Back in Brett's office, Corinne saw the two carriers

sitting on Brett's desk—Alvin peeked out from one, and the one beside him sat empty with the door wide open. "Now, where could your sister be?" she asked the cat.

It yawned.

Corinne got down on her knees and looked under the desk, chairs and couch. She then crawled behind them. She knew the cat was shy and likely would want to find a tight, cozy spot where it couldn't be seen. She looked at the large plant in the corner of the office. That would make a good hiding place. She crept closer.

Alyssa rushed into the room. "What are you doing?"

"Shh...I have to be careful."

Her voice rose in a panic. "We don't have time! Brett will be back soon."

"Actually he's already here," Brett said, standing in the doorway. "What's wrong?"

"Corinne returned to your office without me knowing and knocked Martha's cage," Alyssa said. "Now she's missing." She shot Corinne a look. "I don't know how you could be so careless."

Corinne gaped at her. "What?"

She returned her attention to Brett. "I know I should have called you and told you about the situation, but she begged me not to. I've been trying to help her find Martha before you came back and she—"

Corinne turned away inwardly fuming as Brett's assistant continued her lies. That conniving, horrible woman! She took a deep breath and continued to slowly crawl towards the pot. She didn't care what lies the woman spread about her. All that mattered was finding Martha.

And she did, curled up in the corner, hidden behind the potted plant.

She looked at Brett. He stood with his arms folded and continued listening to his assistant's story. Corinne waved her arm wide to catch his attention, not wanting to shout across the room and scare the cat. He turned to her.

She pointed and mouthed, "She's here."

His expression didn't change but the tension in his posture eased. He walked over to her, bent down and released a breath in relief before he picked up the cat.

"That's lucky," Alyssa said. "You really should be more careful next time."

Corinne gritted her teeth.

"That's enough," Brett said. "You can leave now."

Corinne stood to her feet as the younger woman left. Now she could just return his cell phone and go.

"What were you doing in my office?"

I wasn't in your office, she wanted to say, but wasn't sure he'd believe her. Calling his assistant a liar might not be the best strategy. She pulled out his cell phone from her handbag. "I wanted to return this."

He glanced at the cell phone then turned and placed Martha in her carrier. "Sit down."

"I'd prefer to stand."

He closed the carrier door with a soft click then turned to her, his eyes filled with anger. "Don't ever do that again."

"But I didn't..." She bit her lip. "Okay."

He closed the distance between them. "Do you even know why you're apologizing?"

"Because of my carelessness Martha escaped."

"Really?"

She paused. Was he talking in riddles again?

He took a deep steadying breath, his anger almost palpable. And he was close. So close.

"I'm sorry I upset you this afternoon about pressing you about your past," she said in a quiet voice, "and I'm sorry about—"

"This isn't about Martha."

"It isn't?"

"No, I'm talking about why you took the blame for something you didn't do."

"I'm sorry?"

Brett rested his hands on his hips. "I know you didn't leave the cage open. Alyssa's done it before. It will be her last. I can tolerate some mistakes. I don't tolerate lies. Why didn't you say something?"

"I didn't want...I didn't think you'd believe me."

"Why? You don't trust me?"

"No, it's not that." She felt foolish. Embarrassed that he'd known the truth. Guilty for trying to mislead him. Stupid for standing up for someone who didn't deserve it. Why did this man always seem to catch her at her worst? She lowered her head. "I'm sorry."

He lifted her chin and softened his tone. "Next time tell me the truth. I don't like working with people I don't feel I can trust."

She nodded.

He paused and the expression in his eyes changed. "Corinne, I—"

Her cell phone interrupted him. It was her mother. She'd answer later. "What?"

"Never mind."

"No, please say it."

She waited, the air around them feeling electric, she wondered if he sensed it too.

He opened his mouth then sighed and turned away. "Thanks, for finding her."

Her heart fell, sensing he was about to say something else. "Brett, I think—"

"You should go. Thanks for returning the phone."

He'd closed the door, taking away a chance to get closer. To let her in. She wouldn't cross the line. She turned to leave, feeling his gaze on her back. "Anytime."

CHAPTER TWENTY-TWO

Jason always knew when his dad and stepmother were talking about him. They were never quiet about it. He could comfortably sit on the stairs, rest against the wooden railing and hear them talking in the family room. His Dad's house was much bigger than his mom's and even though he liked his huge bedroom and the indoor swimming pool, he always felt smaller there.

"I didn't sign up for this," his stepmother said. He liked her; he wished she liked him. She still wouldn't let him play with his baby sister even though he'd asked her and told her he would be careful.

"You knew I had a son," his father said. He sounded sad and that made Jason feel sad too.

"I also knew you had an ex-wife who he was supposed to be staying with most of the time. I've got Beth to look after and I don't want to have to pack her up to go to his school because your son doesn't know how to control his temper."

"He's going through a lot right now. I need you to be patient."

"Patient? I think I've been more than patient to have to deal with your other life."

He heard his father sigh. "Corinne and Jason will always be part of my life. My past doesn't just disappear when it's convenient for you. You are my present, my future. I can't choose."

"You did before."

"My relationship with Corinne was already breaking down when we met."

"Yes and you forced me to wait a year before we got married. How long am I supposed to wait until I can feel it's just us?"

His tone hardened. "There's no 'just us'. I told you that Jason comes with the deal."

"Not all the time." Her voice rose to a whine. "It can't be all the time. Talk to her. Tell her that it's not working, tell her that—"

"This is what Jason wants not her."

She sniffed. "So we're supposed to upend our lives for the sake of a seven year old?"

He sighed. "Take a minute to understand."

"No, I don't want to. I'm stressed out as it is. The next time the school calls, he's your problem."

Jason jumped to his feet when he heard her footsteps approach. He hurried to his bedroom and buried himself under the bedcovers.

He squeezed his eyes shut and covered his ears.

A problem. That's all he was. A problem at school. A

problem at home. He didn't want to be a problem anymore.

"It's not working out."

Corinne sat at her kitchen table while her reheated dinner of red beans and rice grew cold. She gripped the phone as she listened to her ex's tired voice. "What do you mean?"

"Jason staying with me. It's not going to work."

"It's barely been three months."

"I know but...Jason got into a fight."

"Jason doesn't get into fights."

"He does now. The school called. I was busy at work so Lily had to go and deal with it." He released a sigh. "Let's say she was less than pleased."

Corinne didn't care. "Is he okay?"

"He's fine, but—"

"Then talk to him. He wants to connect with you anyway."

Harrison sighed again. "With my schedule it will be tough."

"You can find the time. You're not just the fun weekend Dad anymore."

"You're still mad at me."

"I'm not mad, but you were the one who encouraged this. Take responsibility. He's your son."

He hesitated.

"What?"

"Lily is—"

"I don't want to hear it. Is she the queen handing down a royal decree? Isn't it your house too?"

"Beth's been miserable lately. First an ear infection and now teething. We just got word that our housekeeper decided to retire—"

Corinne gasped in mock horror. "Oh my God! Does that mean she'll actually have to...clean? She'll have to touch a-a *sponge*?"

"It's not funny, Corinne."

"Actually it is. The sight of Lily holding a duster or washing dishes is quite a funny thought. Then again she could turn it into a workout routine."

He sighed again. "I just need you to take him while I arrange my schedule so I can talk to him about school. Please."

Harrison rarely said "please" so she knew he was desperate. Lily was probably driving him crazy. "Okay. I'll see what I can do next week."

He hesitated. "Actually, I need to drop him off tomorrow."

"What? That's in the middle of a school week. Why not wait—"

"He's been suspended for two days. Lily planned to see her sister and can't look after him and I can hardly take him to work with me."

Brett's workshop was this Friday. She'd managed to keep her distance from him for weeks. She'd already upset him by hinting at his past and lying about losing Martha. How would it be if she showed up with a surly seven year old in tow? "I can't. I have a major event coming up. You know how crazy my days can be."

"This is an emergency."

"No, it's not. Lily can visit her sister another time."

"You're being petty."

"*I'm* being petty? This is my livelihood we're talking about."

"You're the one who didn't want him living with me full-time. This is your chance to prove that you're the right choice."

She fell silent. "That's how you do it."

"What?"

"That's how you've always done it. The moment I feel like I'm getting myself together you drop a bomb in my life."

"Don't be dramatic," he said as if he were talking to a petulant child.

"You're always dropping little bombs in my life. You asked for a divorce and made it seem like it was all my fault. I wasn't giving you enough time, I was too focused on my business, on Jason, you felt unloved. You always make me feel bad. You always come up with an argument that puts me on the defense."

"Corinne—"

"But I didn't fight you. I gave you what you wanted. Only a few months ago I gave in again. You came up with the reasons why Jason should stay with you and I said he could be with you for six months."

"I don't—"

"And you *knew* how hard it was for me to make that decision. But I wanted Jason to be happy. I wanted to work hard on my business so that when he was with me again things would be different. And finally, I feel like

I'm getting my life back on track. I have an important event coming up and now you're ready with another bomb. Now you're telling me having Jason with you is inconvenient; you're coming up with reasons it can't work because that's how you operate. The moment things start getting difficult you bail. You don't give me a chance to fight back."

"This isn't a fight."

"Then why didn't you tell me Jason was having trouble at school? Why didn't you call me before?"

"I didn't think it would get this bad. I didn't plan any of this. You know how Lily can be when she—"

"Doesn't get her way? I really was a doormat. No wonder you lost interest in me. I should have been more demanding."

"Can't he stay with your parents?" he asked and she heard the pleading in his voice.

"They're out of town. They won't be back until next week."

"You can make this work. You've done it before. I promise I'll make this up to you. I'm begging you. *Please.*"

It was time to pull out her second pair of stockings. Before she'd left the Wildfire Spa Rania had suggested she wear the floral fishnets when she was ready for a fight.

She was ready for one now. She wouldn't let Harrison get to her. She wouldn't pretend that she wasn't angry. That she didn't feel guilty. She loved her son. She never wanted to think of him as an inconvenience, but the timing of everything certainly was.

However, she'd gotten this far. Over the past several months she'd faced a number of fears.

She'd gone back to the Wildfire Spa after avoiding it for years.

She'd put on a skirt again, more than once, and worn stockings that drew attention to her legs. It had been the same pair, but she hadn't been ready to try the others yet.

She'd made a decision and given Harrison and Jason a six month trial period.

She'd pitched to the owner of Quest.

Corinne opened her bedroom closet, reached for the top shelf and took down the box where she kept the remaining pair of stockings. She rested the box on her bed and opened it.

She took a deep breath before she took out the floral fishnets. Only a few months ago she could never imagine herself wearing something like this.

But now it felt right. She felt strong enough to try.

She was a woman who wouldn't be cowed by her ex's manipulation. She wouldn't let this latest bomb destroy her. She'd admit to being shaken, to even being a little scared, but she wouldn't fall. She would remain standing.

CHAPTER TWENTY-THREE

IN ALL HIS thirty-five years Brett had see a lot of things. But he'd never seen a child filled with rage.

It wasn't easy to see. Not at first. Especially for him. When Brett first spotted Corinne in the main entrance of the mansion he'd been taken by the sight of her. He knew today was important to her as the event planner, and she looked radiant and fierce wearing a burgundy long sleeved shift dress, perfect for the bright May morning, and a pair of sexy black stockings with a flower pattern that made him question why he hadn't just grabbed and kissed her when he'd had a chance in his office.

But then Corinne introduced him to her son, Jason, and he had to tuck away any images of her dress hiked up to her waist and the feel of her legs wrapped around him. She apologized for having to bring her son with her due to a scheduling mix-up with her ex and Brett quickly assured her that it was okay.

He'd already been impressed by how the team she'd

hired had transformed his simple workshop idea into an innovative creative experience. The workshop space boasted two large screens; comfortable seating with small group table settings to allow for interaction, plus the catering crew had already prepared a lavish breakfast buffet the attendees were enjoying with enthusiasm. He felt certain things would be fine.

AND AT FIRST it seemed that way. All Brett saw was a cute kid with a ready smile, but it was in one flash moment that he saw something in Jason's eyes. His eyes told a different story. His eyes were guarded and angry.

Brett knew all about anger. Understood it. He understood its many forms and shades. Especially young anger, the most destructive kind because it was fresh and raw and knew no outlet because it wasn't seen.

He couldn't imagine how Jason felt being shuffled between parents. But he sensed something was wrong and that Jason didn't have the language yet to understand his own feelings; to know that sometimes the people you love the most were the ones who could leave you with the most scars. That there were so many things in life that you couldn't control; that being a good kid wasn't good enough and being a bad kid won't always get you the real attention you crave.

Brett kept his observation to himself. He didn't ask her why Jason was out of school or why she seemed so frazzled to have him there. He'd seen her nervous, terrified, angry, but never frazzled. He doubted her story about a parenting mix-up, but it wasn't his place to pry.

But throughout the morning he watched Jason with interest.

Everything about him was typical. The way he flopped in a chair, shrugged when his mother asked him a question, once he even grinned at her, but Brett sensed it was all an act. When Corinne wasn't looking, Brett caught Jason watching her, studying her, seeing how his actions impacted her. Brett sensed the boy wanted something from his mother. He couldn't guess what, but he saw a brief expression of longing that he knew only too well.

During the lunch break Brett called his father before he sat down beside Jason and was greeted with a dark look, but knew the anger wasn't directed at him. He saw the child's fear—a fear that he would be replaced in his mother's affection, but he was also afraid of making her upset.

Such a heavy weight on a little boy's shoulders. Brett couldn't fix things, but he could distract him for a little while.

He looked out at the crowd, pretending to be disinterested with the young boy sitting beside him before he nudged him with his elbow. The boy pulled off his headphones and stared at him curious.

"I need your help," Brett said in a low voice, keeping his gaze focused on the crowd.

"What?"

He turned to him. "Can you help me?"

"Me?"

"Yes, it's a very important job. Are you up to it?"

"I-I don't know."

"Your mom told me you're smart and that I can trust you. Is she right?"

"I-I guess so."

"Good."

"My father is a volunteer at a local animal shelter and they're doing a big fundraiser. Do you know what that is?"

He shook his head.

"It's an event where they raise money. Anyway, he needs an assistant to help him promote it. They have to design a poster, but the person who was supposed to help got sick and now there might not be a fundraiser and the shelter might have to shut down. If they close then no one can take care of the animals."

Jason's eyes widened. "What will happen to them?"

Brett shrugged, sad.

His eyes started to fill with tears. "Will they have to kill them?"

"No," Brett said quickly. "Not if you can help."

"What can I do?"

"You can draw, right?" he asked even though he already knew the answer. He'd seen Jason drawing with colored pencils.

He nodded vigorously.

"Great. When my Dad gets here he's going to bring some poster board and I need you to draw three posters. He'll do the lettering—"

Jason frowned. "The letter-what?"

"He'll write the words. All you have to do is draw the

picture. Can you do that for us? Can we trust you to give us your best?"

"Yes. Yes."

"And if you like cats, I could use someone to play with mine sometimes."

"I like cats."

"Good." He noticed his father coming through the entrance and waved. "Here's my Dad now." When his father reached them he stood and said, "Dad this is Jason. The young man who is going to assist you with that very special project we discussed." He sent his father a silent message.

His father bit back a grin before he said, "Yes, I'm glad you found someone to help me. I know a place where we can set up and get to work. Well then young man, follow me."

"Okay." Jason grabbed his bag.

"Wait. We have to ask your Mom first."

Jason shifted from side to side eager to leave. "She won't mind. She'll know—"

"Stay here." Brett walked over to Corinne who was talking to the A/V person and said, "Please just smile at your son and nod your head, I'll explain later."

"What?"

"Smile and nod."

She hesitated then did so. Jason smiled back then followed Brett's father out the door.

"Wait," Corinne said, heading after him. "Where is he going?"

Brett grabbed her arm. "It's okay. I've given him a job."

"A job?"

"Yes, he's helping my dad with an imaginary fundraiser I just came up with. It's another event I'll have to hire you to set up for me, but it's worth it," he said with a chuckle. "It will keep him occupied. Don't worry, my Dad's good with kids."

"But—"

"Please, he needs this," Brett said. He knew Corinne would think he meant his father but he didn't want to explain the truth.

CHAPTER TWENTY-FOUR

"And he said my posters could help to save them!" Jason gushed as Corinne drove him home. Although it was late he was still full of energy. He'd talked almost non-stop about the afternoon he'd spent with Brett's father, talking about the movie they'd watched together and the game they'd played on his game tablet, the chicken nuggets they'd had for dinner, but most importantly the drawing and posters they'd worked on together to save the animal shelter.

She listened to her son amazed. She hadn't seen Jason so animated in a long time.

She was glad for the chatter. At least she didn't have to fill the silence, plus his enthusiasm made it easier to not think about what had happened only ten minutes ago.

She'd expected to leave the workshop feeling exhausted, a little sad, but relieved that the event had been successful. Instead Brett...

"And Mr. Lattimore said he liked them all..."

She took a deep breath. First she had to calm down. She had to get home and get Jason ready for bed and later call Harrison about next week.

"He showed me pictures of his cats..."

Then she'd think about the yellow sticky note Brett had put on the back of her hand, as she was tying up the event. She sometimes received handshakes, hugs or thank you notes at the conclusion of an event but never something like this. She'd glanced at it wondering what she might have forgotten...

At first she'd stood there. She didn't think the bold scribbled note was real. He'd been so casual about giving it to her. She read it slowly to make sure she hadn't misunderstood.

If you like vanilla almond tarts, I make the best. A token of my thanks. Plenty of food and dessert. My place next Saturday 7PM.

She blinked. The words remained the same. She hadn't misread them. He was inviting her out. He was going to cook for her. Really? Corinne had looked up to try to catch his eye, but he was talking to one of the attendees. He was only a few feet from her but felt miles away. She wondered if she was reading too much into it. It was merely a token of thanks, right?

She looked at the note again. Her racing heart told her it meant much more. When he finished his conversation, she rushed up to him, but before he could say anything his assistant tapped his shoulder and reminded him he needed talk to one of the speakers who was getting ready to leave.

"Thank you," he told the assistant before he turned to Corinne and said in a businesslike tone, "Is that an event you think you can attend?"

She blinked. Her mind racing. An event? Was she supposed to do another event for him? Another one besides the animal shelter fundraiser? Brett blinked and she briefly saw his gaze drop to the note in her hand. She realized he didn't want anyone else to know about it, but wanted to confirm her reply.

"Yes," she said quickly. "Yes of course."

"There won't be a scheduling conflict?"

She knew he was asking about Jason and appreciated that. "No, my schedule is free."

"Good." He left the room.

She read the note three more times. He wanted to cook for her. He wanted to have her come over to his place and cook for her? This was beyond anything she could have ever imagined.

"Isn't that great Mom?" she heard Jason say.

Corinne grinned. "Yes, it's wonderful."

"He asked you out?" Vivian stared at Corinne amazed. "Are you sure?"

It had been nearly a week since the Quest workshop, five days since she'd had a talk with Jason and he'd clammed up about why he'd gotten into fights at school; four days since she got him to talk to her again about another drawing he wanted to do for the shelter; three days since she'd had a fight with Harrison about Jason spending another week with her (she told him no), and one day since she'd called Vivian to come over and help her select something to wear for Saturday.

Vivian sat on Corinne's bed and shook her head. "Are you sure?"

"Of course I'm sure."

"It's just he doesn't seem the kind of man who dates."

"What do you think he does in his spare time?"

"Men like him don't usually have any. You're certain he—"

"Yes."

She didn't want to show her the sticky note and felt even guilty that she'd said anything. Brett seemed to want to keep their date a secret, but she wanted Vivian to help her choose something to wear.

"Just don't be disappointed if it turns out to be a business dinner or something."

"I won't. But promise not to tell anyone."

Vivian bit her lip. "Are you really sure—"

"I'm sure!"

She held up her hands. "Okay, okay." She sighed. "I knew you two would get on professionally, but I really didn't think it would lead to this. Remember, he still can be as cuddly as a porcupine."

"I know."

"But he certainly is a big change from Harrison if that's what you're after."

Corinne looked through her closet. "Right now all I'm after is the right dress to wear," she said glad Rania had convinced her to take more than the one dress and two skirts she'd planned on when she'd had a chance at the Wildfire Spa. She now had seven. "I have two I'm thinking of."

"I'm still in shock that you're thinking of wearing a dress. I don't think I've ever seen you in a dress."

"I wore one to the Quest workshop."

"Yes, well I wasn't at the workshop, was I?"

"Doesn't matter. This is important and I have my reasons." She reached inside her closet and pulled out two different dresses—one a blue flare dress the other a red V-neck—and held them up. "Which one?"

Vivian studied them then pointed. "Go with the red."

"Blue it is."

"I said red."

"I know, that's why I'm going with blue. I don't want to come on too strong."

"I don't think you can, although you have changed a lot lately. It's nice to see you taking a risk like this. First you pitch to Brett Lattimore, manage to hook him and now you're going out with him."

"You make me sound devious."

"Might make it awkward to get more business from him if things don't work out."

Corinne made a face. "Now you're beginning to sound like Bonnie."

Vivian shivered and slapped her mouth. "Forget I said anything."

"I know things could get complicated. I know that if this dinner goes south I could lose potential leads or referrals."

Vivian grinned. "But you don't care?"

Corinne smiled back. "Not one bit."

"You like him that much?

"Yes." She even knew the third pair of stockings she would wear.

Vivian shook her head amazed. "You certainly have changed."

"I know and it feels good."

CHAPTER TWENTY-FIVE

BRETT CHOPPED, he sautéed, he baked, he set the table and he waited.

And waited.

He waited until two o'clock and then checked his phone for any missed messages. Nothing. He waited another half hour and another. Not believing what was truly happening. Not to him. She hadn't done this to him, had she?

He looked at his cell phone. Perhaps something had happened? He started to call Corinne then stopped. He didn't know what to say. He didn't want to sound pathetic. What if she'd changed her mind and was too afraid to tell him? What if she'd forgotten? Somehow knowing that was infinitely worse, it meant she cared so little for him that her offhanded "yes" had been meant to just get him off her back.

He set his phone down on the counter. If she wanted to forget it, he would to. He'd pretend it never happened.

He'd never written the note; he'd never stuck it on the back of her hand. He'd never told his father he'd taken a risk. He'd never spent the last week preparing for this day.

He put the dishes away, more carefully than usual to get over the urge to throw them on the ground and shatter every plate and drinking glass. He could afford to replace them. But no, he wouldn't let her upset him and cost him more than she already had. It wasn't the food. He'd give it away. No, it was his time, it was the hope she'd offered him. He'd never forgive her for taking that away.

He dropped the food off at his parents' house, not giving them a chance to ask any questions. He didn't care if they ate it, threw it or gave it away. He returned home and completed some dynamic stretching routines to limber up his body, but he still felt tense so he went for a run. He came back, showered and sat on the couch and read over a report.

He squeezed his eyes shut. He hurt. He hurt so bad. He'd almost let her in. He'd almost let her get close and she'd...

He heard a soft cry and looked down at Alvin and Martha. It hurt too much to bend down and stroke them.

The pain burned. He wished he hadn't listened to his father. It all should have ended that day. The workshop had been a success. He should have trusted his instincts.

He grabbed a jump rope and did some more exercises then showered again until his skin felt like rubber. Now he could focus. He'd helped people. His employees seemed happy. He'd think of a similar event for next year.

Work was something that kept his mind occupied.

He could find problems to solve. The business needed him; its survival depended on him. He needed to feel needed. Otherwise there was nothing else to keep him together, to keep him facing each new day.

When the doorbell rang at seven o'clock he paused. He wasn't expecting anyone.

He looked through the peephole. His heart constricted. It couldn't be.

No. No. It couldn't be! Brett turned from the door, leaning his back against it as the bell rang again. She had the nerve to show up six hours late? Was she drunk?

He took a deep breath turned and gripped the handle.

He swung the door open and before he could speak Corinne flashed a wide smile and held out three large Asian pears.

"I heard they were your favorite," she said.

They were. She'd even gotten the brand right. And she looked beautiful in a blue dress and wearing animal print stockings.

What was going on? He gripped the door handle, not trusting himself to speak. Anger and relief warred within him. And it angered him even more how relieved he felt that she'd come at all. Was this some sort of test? That's what his ex Delaney always did with him. Loving her was exhausting. She always found ways that he had to prove his interest in her. She'd arrive late for dates and kiss him and say, "If you loved me you'd understand", or miss a meeting and say the same. He'd twisted himself into loops for her. But he wouldn't do it now.

Never again. Ever. He hadn't thought Corinne would

be like that. He thought she was more honest. If he let her walk through the door would that be a triumph for her, to show she could control him? That she had him wrapped around her finger? He should close the door in her face. Why wasn't he? Why had he weakened at the sight of that smile?

She frowned. "What's wrong?" She looked down at his jeans and shirt. "Did I come on the wrong day?"

Brett bit his lip and shook his head before he motioned her inside.

She tentatively entered, sending him a wary look. "Am I overdressed? I know we're not going out but I thought...?"

He took a deep breath and slowly closed the door. "You look nice." It was all he could manage without revealing how he really felt. He was still angry and needed to gain control. She could never know how much she affected him. At least the place gave no sign to all the effort he'd gone through—the dining table lay bare, not a single item in the kitchen was out of place.

"Hello," she said in greeting when Alvin came to inspect. She opened her handbag, pulled out a pouch and shook it. "I brought you a treat too." Brett's heart shifted at the bright smile on her face as she tucked the pouch back in her handbag, but when Martha shyly brushed Corinne's hand and she gently scratched the cat behind its ears, he felt his temper rise. How could she pretend to be so kind? He turned. If he shouted at her, she'd know how he felt. "Excuse me."

"I surprised you, didn't I?" she said, rising to her feet.

"You're used to women who are late. But I told you I'm always punctual."

He spun around and glared at her. "Punctual? You call this punctual?"

"Yes," Corinne said, the light in her eyes dimming. "Seven on the dot."

"Seven?" His voice cracked; his heart started to race. "Seven?"

"Y-yes, that's what you wrote."

He ran a hand down his face and marched to the kitchen. "I don't believe this."

She set the pears on the kitchen table and began to search in her handbag.

He watched her. "What are you doing?"

"Looking for the note."

"You kept it?"

"Of course I kept it."

"I thought you'd read it and throw it away."

"Why would I do that? But where...yes, here it is. My place. Seven o'clock," she read.

Brett held out his hand. "Can I see that?"

"Sure." She started to hand it to him then stopped. "Wait." Her eyes widened. "You didn't send this to me, did you? Was this some mistake? A colossal joke? Did you mean to give me something else?" She looked down at the note. "It looks like your handwriting, but maybe someone copied it and—"

"I wrote it and gave it to you. It wasn't a mistake," he said impatient. He wiggled his fingers. "Let me see it."

She handed the sticky note to him.

Brett looked at it then held it up for her to see. He pointed to the number. "This is a one!"

She frowned. "A one?"

He nodded.

"Not a seven?"

He shook his head.

She looked at him for a moment then a slow realization crossed her face before it was replaced by a look of horror. "Oh no. I was supposed to come for *lunch* not dinner?"

He nodded.

"I'm so sorry." She snatched the note from him and frantically scanned it. "I was so certain it was a seven. I should have verified."

"It's my fault. I should have made it clear." Vivian had warned him about his handwriting.

"Did you cook?"

Brett folded his arms and leaned against the counter. He bit his lip. He could lie. He could tell her that he'd changed his mind and planned to order in so it wasn't a big deal. But right now he had to get away from her because he wasn't angry anymore. He was relieved. So relieved that she hadn't forgotten, that she hadn't made him wait on purpose, that she had come. He had a wild urge to hug her. That wasn't a good thing. Not yet.

He turned. "Let me change and we can go out somewhere." He didn't give her a chance to say anything before he left the kitchen.

He went into the bathroom and turned on the shower, but didn't get inside. Instead he paced his bedroom. He shouldn't be this happy, but damn he was.

He hadn't made an idiot of himself. She was here and she looked wonderful. He could salvage this. The risk had been worth it.

He changed into a long sleeve green shirt and a pair of dark trousers and found her sitting at the kitchen table staring at the Asian pears with a sad expression. He didn't want to see her sad.

He pulled out a chair and sat in front of her. "If you're willing to wait, I can cook something."

"I wish you had called me. Or sent a text."

"Saying what?"

"I don't know...telling me you were waiting."

"I'm not your boss. Or a client."

"But this was a date, right?"

He shrugged. "I was too proud."

"What does pride have to do with anything?"

He rubbed the back of his neck. "I thought you'd changed your mind."

She groaned and hung her head. "What a kerfuffle."

"What?"

She lifted her head. "Never mind."

Brett stood. "Where do you want to go?"

Corinne shook her head. "No, I can wait for you to cook something. I was thinking about it all week."

He bit his lip again, this time trying hard to stop a smile. He hated how pleased that made him feel. "Okay, but I have to get some items."

"I can help."

He grabbed a notepad and wrote some ingredients down. "You go here and pick up these items. I have another place I have to go. We'll meet back at my place, okay?" He pulled out his wallet and handed her some money.

She waved it away. "I already cost you the first round, I can do this."

CORINNE SWORE as she walked to her car. The evening air was warm with the promise of a coming summer, but her skin burned as if she'd been thrown inside a volcano. How could she have gotten the time wrong? Six hours late! No wonder he'd looked furious. She was shocked he'd even let her inside. If it had been her, she would have shouted at him then shoved a pear in his mouth.

He'd thought she'd changed her mind? Without telling him? Who did he think she was?

She looked at the items on the list. The shop he'd recommended was expensive and her debit card would cry a bit, but it was worth it. The Quest workshop had been lucrative enough to carry her through a couple months. Plus, she knew she was lucky he was giving her a second chance in the first place. She didn't want to blow it. A man like Brett wasn't easy to win over and she planned to win him completely.

CHAPTER TWENTY-SIX

Brett arrived back at the house before Corinne. He was putting a tomato on the cutting board when he realized he'd made a mistake. He always cooked *before* guests arrived; he'd learned that lesson after Delaney. He knew it was best that no one saw his methods so that they couldn't criticize them. "You look so serious," she liked to tease him. "Are you having any fun at all?"

And Corinne could be worse. She liked to watch him. He knew that. She had once said she liked the way he moved, but when he cooked he was different. He wasn't elegant or smooth. Sometimes he dropped things, twice he'd cut his finger. His meals always came out well, but they took effort. He wasn't ready for her to see that side yet.

Perhaps he should turn on the TV and let her get lost in a show to distract her. Yes, that would be best.

The doorbell rang and he let her in. He took the

grocery bags from her and motioned to the living room TV but before he could say anything she said, "Let me go wash my hands then I can help you."

"I don't need help," he said following her, wondering how he could stop her.

"I'm great with chopping."

"But—"

"It will get things done faster, don't you think? And I'm starving."

"Then we could order in."

"All right, okay, I won't exaggerate. I'm just hungry," she corrected. She went over to the sink and washed her hands.

He sighed and turned to the stove.

"Wait!"

"What?"

"Where's your apron?"

He pointed to the pantry. She grabbed the apron then returned to him and said, "Bend down a little so that I can put this on you. I'd hate for you to get oil or food on your nice shirt." She tied the back string. "Okay, you're the chef now."

"What about you? I don't have another—"

"It's okay. I'll be careful."

But Brett didn't like the idea of her ruining her dress so he went to his bedroom and came back with a light red shirt she could wear to protect her dress. "It's a little big," he said, which was an understatement. When she put it on it swallowed her, the sleeves falling past her hands.

"It's perfect." She buttoned up the shirt and rolled up the sleeves. "What do you want me to do?"

He wasn't quite sure. She'd helped him put on the apron as if she *expected* him to be messy and didn't care. He felt his tension ease. There was no need to be on guard. She was easy to get along with, easy to work with. He should have known that from their professional relationship, but he still found this moment surprising. No criticisms, no impatience.

She was here in his kitchen, eager to help him, looking beautiful...

"Chef?"

It took him a moment to realize he was staring at her.

He motioned to the cutting board where he had added some carrots.

"I want slices, not too fat or thin."

She gave him a mock salute. "I'm on it." She lifted the knife. "I'm glad I came, even though I was late."

"Just get chopping," he said, which was the best way he could manage *I'm glad you came too*, without saying the words.

THE ALMOND VANILLA tart was pure heaven on a plate. Corinne leaned back from the dining table and closed her eyes as she finished her last bite. "This was delicious."

"Of course."

She opened her eyes and licked her fork. "I thought you were making an empty boast."

Brett tried not to follow the movement of her tongue, imagining its warm, pink tip licking him. "I never boast. But you can cook for me next time."

She set the fork down and shook her head. "After this, anything would be a colossal failure in comparison."

"I doubt that. You helped after all."

"Cutting vegetables and stirring batter doesn't really count."

He pushed the remainder of his tart across the table to her. "You met my specifications."

She eagerly accepted it. "Meeting your specifications has become a challenge of mine, remember?" She lifted her fork and took another bite.

A faint smile touched his lips. "I do. You're one of the few who hasn't run away."

"I did the first time," she said, reminding him of their first official meeting in the conference room.

"But you came back."

She nodded. "That's true."

He rested his chin in his hand. "Why? You needed the money?"

"I'd never admit that to you."

"I'm curious."

She pointed down to the tart in front of her. "It will take a lot more than this to get me to make myself that transparent."

"Fair enough."

"Do you like scaring people?"

He thought for a moment. "I don't do it on purpose, but it's been effective. People rarely waste my time. When they do, they never do so again."

"Your time is that important?"

"I think any limited resource is."

"A limited resource," Corinne said with a laugh. "Only you could say something like that and sound sincere."

He held her gaze and his voice deepened. "Because I am and being the smart woman you are I hope you understand even more."

She set her fork down and blinked. "Even more?"

"How much this dinner really costs."

She groaned. "Yes, I wasted six hours of your time."

He bit his lip, leaned forward. "No, that's not what I meant. I mean...I'd like to spend more time with you."

She knew how difficult it was for him to say those words and she didn't know how to respond. Saying "me too" seemed so simple and didn't say what she truly felt. "I'm afraid I can't—"

He leaned back in his chair. "I see."

"Be completely free right now. I have a son."

"I know that."

"And he's living with his father now and I hope...it's complicated but he's part of my life and I don't want to continue this if that would be a problem for you."

"I wouldn't have asked you here if it would be." Brett studied her for a moment before he said, "I was surprised you had a child though."

"Why?"

"Because at the train station you were going to—"

"I wasn't going to do anything," she cut in. "I was just thinking about it. Why do you have to keep bringing it up?" She pushed back her chair. "Maybe...maybe this isn't a good idea after all."

"I want to understand how a mother could—"

"Think that her son would be better off without her? Her ex too? How she could imagine how much easier his life would be if he didn't have to choose between the two? If the choice was made for him? How she could imagine a simple burial, a few tears shed for her and then be lost to memory? How her son would only know that she'd been involved in an accident, that she'd leave no note so that there could be no thought of suicide?

"How this woman would wrap herself in all her sorrow, let the darkness of her thoughts, thoughts that won't leave her, thoughts that grow blacker with each day, and throw herself into the path of release?" Corinne gripped her hands into fists. "It was a moment of weakness. A moment I wish you'd never seen. A moment that I'm ashamed anyone witnessed, but a moment I needed because I needed to face my pain, my fear. When you're alone. No, that's not right. When you *feel* alone. Truly alone...that moment of agony is so acute you just want it to end by any means. That's the woman you saw that day. I can't pretend she won't come back, that I won't waver, that I'm as strong as you, but if you can't accept that then I have wasted your precious time and I won't do it anymore."

Brett stared at her for a long moment and she saw judgment in his gaze before he lowered it. Her heart fell. He wasn't safe. He wasn't someone who could understand her. Someone she could trust.

"You don't know your power," he said in a soft voice.

"I'm sorry?"

"You call yourself weak, pathetic, but you're wrong.

You don't know how truly powerful you are and that's what frightens me. Reckless power. You have no idea how many lives you impact. The carnage you'd leave behind." He lifted his dark gaze to capture and hold hers. "Perhaps I'm the weak one. Perhaps I'm the one who's not as strong as he should be because I can't risk...I couldn't face...I'm not..." He took a deep, steadying breath. "I want to be with you. I want to sleep with you. But I will not go through that again. I don't want to worry that if we have an argument you might try—"

"I won't."

"Promise me. Promise me that much. On the life of your son promise me."

Corinne stared at him, shocked by the pain in his voice. "Who was it?"

"Promise me."

"How old were you?"

"I said—"

"No, I won't promise you."

He stared at her uncertain. "Why not?"

"I won't promise because you won't believe me. You won't let go. Just as you won't let go of that moment and I won't spend my time trying to convince you to trust me. I'm not fragile like glass, if you're worried I'll break then perhaps we shouldn't be talking at all. I can tell you this much. I have dark moments, I think dark thoughts, but I want to see my son grow up, I want to run my business and I want to be with you too. I thought about you all week. I've dreamed about you. I want to get to know all about you. I lost myself for a long time and I'm...recreating myself. I'm not going to do anything rash and I'm not going anywhere. That's all I can promise you."

Brett released a long sigh. "I see."

Corinne swallowed her heart heavy. "It's not enough, is it?"

"No."

She stood, defeated. She'd tried and it had all been wasted. The clothes, the food, the speech. Vivian had warned her about his boundaries. About his guard. She hadn't been able to penetrate them. She hadn't won at all.

"But it will have to be," Brett said in a soft voice. A voice so soft it felt like a caress.

She met his gaze.

He stood and held out his hand. "Because I want this more than anything. Come. I have to show you something."

She hesitated. "How old were you when..."

He shook his head. "I don't want to talk about that right now."

"Okay." She took his hand and the moment they touched she felt a warm shiver course through her.

One day she wanted to ask him more, but knew better than to press him. They'd both already revealed more than they'd expected to. Part of her wanted to run from this solid, intense man and hide. How could she have said things she'd never told anyone else? What did he really think of her? Did it matter? She was still here. She looked down at his hand. He held hers so causally in his hand she'd forgotten about it. That surprised her. She'd expected a man like him to have a possessive, tight grasp that made it impossible not to notice. But no, his clasp was strangely tender, comforting. What pain had he gone through? She hoped she'd get to know in time so that she could comfort him in return.

She let him lead her to the living room; she hadn't left the kitchen since she'd arrived. She'd been too afraid to make another wrong move and ruin whatever relationship they were building. She didn't want to see what he didn't want her to.

Once there she looked around the room expecting it to be similar to his office, but it wasn't. It was more classically comfortable with a grey couch and a hand woven Moroccan rug—their color tones matching the large black and white poster of three male dancers, facing the camera, doing a split in mid air. She pointed and gasped when she recognized the person to the right. "It's you! You *are* a dancer."

"I *was* a dancer. Many years ago. Tap and street."

She walked closer to the poster impressed by the power of the pose. "Oh my goodness you were so young." She turned to him. "Why did you stop?"

Brett glanced away and she sensed he'd shut the door on that topic. "I didn't bring you in here to see that." He pointed to another large photograph. "What do you think?"

She saw the profile of a lioness resting in the grass. "It's a beautiful picture."

"A friend of mine took that picture while on a trip to South Africa and gave it to me as a gift. She's my favorite animal. A lioness has no mane, but she has no need of one. She has nothing to prove, every action shows her warrior spirit. She works with others when needed, provides for her young. A fierce, beautiful creature."

"I'm surprised. I thought you would have chosen the lion, who is usually alone."

"No," Brett said in a raw whisper, turning her to him. "That's the problem. I don't want to be alone," and he showed her the strength of his feelings by pressing his lips to hers.

CHAPTER TWENTY-SEVEN

Somehow she had expected this. Wanted this. Wanted to feel this man's lips on hers, to feel the heat of his body against hers. She didn't think it would happen tonight, she'd dreamt it might, but she'd imagined they would have had a few more dates before this moment.

But this moment, this heavenly moment was perfect. She already felt ripped bare so all her senses felt extra heightened—the scent of him (vanilla), the feel of him (smooth), the taste of him (sweet). How could a man with such hard eyes, guarded emotions, enigmatic expressions, how could this guarded man have such a soft—buttery soft—mouth? How could it feel so right to be in his arms?

"Come with me," he growled then led her to his bedroom where he drew her close again and let his mouth leave a trail of sizzling kisses down her neck.

His hot hands made a searing descent down her hip and slid to her thigh. She froze. She moved his hand and placed it back on her waist. After a few seconds his hand made another dangerous descent and she pushed it back up.

Brett drew back and stared at her confused. "What are you doing?"

She grinned and toyed with one of the buttons of his shirt. "Do I really need to explain it to you?"

He didn't smile back. "You don't like me to touch you?"

"Anywhere but the thighs."

His eyebrows shot up. "You're kidding, right?"

"Those are the rules."

He slowly blinked. "There are rules?"

"Yes. You can touch me anywhere—"

"But the thighs."

She nodded.

"But I like them the best," he said like a kid being denied his favorite toy.

She pushed away from him. "Very funny."

"I'm not kidding. What's wrong with your thighs?"

"You know what's wrong...please don't pretend..." Corinne took a deep breath. "Can't we just finish what we were doing?"

"In case you were wondering, I want to sleep with you."

She leaned in close and whispered, "I believe that's why we're here," she said glancing around his bedroom.

He held her back. "That means I want to roll up your skirt, pull down your stockings and get between your thighs."

"Which you can do later, when it's dark—"

He swore. "If you don't want to do this, just say so."

"I am saying so. You're the one who isn't listening." She grabbed the front of his shirt. "Just follow my lead and I'll show you." She kissed him again, stopping any protest. She unbuttoned his shirt; he unzipped her dress, it fell to the floor revealing her black slip.

He frowned at the sight of it. "What's that? It's blocking my view of your—"

"Which is exactly the point. Plus it controls static cling, especially with stockings."

"Good to know. Now let's—" He reached for her slip.

She stopped him. "I'll remove it later." She pushed him backwards and they fell on the bed. His hand slid down her hip towards her thigh, she removed it. He made a growl of protest but didn't argue.

She rolled off her stockings and dove under the covers, before she shimmied out of her slip, while Brett stripped out of his clothes. But when he got in bed beside her and started to lift the covers to get a better look at her, she snatched them away and said, "Look at me."

He tugged at the covers. "I'm trying to."

"I mean my face."

He shifted his gaze. "I am looking."

"Good. Keep your gaze there and let your body do the rest."

"You're not serious?"

"I'm perfectly serious." She reached for him. "Do you need me to guide you?"

"No."

"Good." She kissed him again. The feel of his bare body touching hers made her wet with wanting. She moaned against his lips.

He groaned then he drew back and shook his head. "I can't do it like this."

"Want to switch positions?" she said breathless, eager to feel him close again.

"I want to touch you."

"You are."

"*Everywhere.*"

She clenched her teeth. Why was he being so stubborn? "I don't ask for much." She bit her lip. "Please understand I'm very conscious about my flaws."

"What flaws?" He pulled back the sheets revealing her bare lower half.

She screamed in outrage and grabbed the sheets. "What is wrong with you?"

"There's nothing wrong with me or with you."

Corinne stared at him, her voice filled with hurt. "Since you clearly don't understand boundaries, I should go."

Brett sighed. "You've got great legs."

"Lying doesn't help."

"I'm not lying."

"You're saying I have gorgeous, slender legs."

"No."

"So you were lying."

"No," he said again, slowly. "You do have great legs. Beautiful, curvy legs."

"Thick legs like tree trunks."

Brett ran a hand down his face and mumbled. "I can't believe I'm having this conversation."

"Then let's not." She wiggled on her slip.

"You're telling me you come here wearing sexy animal print stockings and you don't like your legs?"

She picked her dress up from off the floor. "I did it because I had to."

"Why?"

"It doesn't matter now."

He came up behind her and whispered, "I happen to like your legs. I find them very attractive. You don't have to tease me like this."

"I'm not teasing."

He placed a warm, wet kiss on the back of her neck. "All the stockings you've been wearing—"

"There aren't that many."

"Weren't to impress me?"

She sighed. She couldn't tell him that she'd been forced to. She had to admit that she'd gotten used to wearing them, but without them she was reminded of how ordinary she was.

"Indulge me," Brett said in a low silky voice, turning her to face him. "You may not like your legs, but I do. Let me introduce myself."

"In-introduce yourself?"

"Yes." He gently pushed her back, forcing her to sit on the edge of the bed then knelt down in front of her. His gaze swept down her lower half with admiration. "Corinne's beautiful legs you don't know how long I've wanted to be this close to you."

"Brett—"

He lifted his gaze and shot her a look. "Excuse me, but this is a private conversation."

He slowly ran one large hand up her calf then along her inner thigh, filling her body with sweet anticipation. "I'm looking forward to getting better acquainted," he said in a husky whisper. "I'm sorry it took this long." He pressed his warm mouth against the tender skin of one thigh and then the other before he cupped the back of her thigh. "You're like a juicy papaya in my hand. Sweet, ripe, full, succulent." He pressed his lips against her thigh and sucked her skin before she felt the wet tip of his tongue. "So delicious."

"You're being ridiculous," Corinne said, feeling aroused and breathless. "They used to call me thunder thighs at school."

Brett's eyes met hers. But it was the expression in them that shocked her. His gaze smoldered. Making her body turn hot and wet.

His expression stilled; an eager note entered his voice. "Are you serious?"

Corinne licked her lips unsure of his response, unsure why the look in his eyes made her senses spin. "Y-yes."

Brett slowly rose to his feet, his intense gaze never leaving her face. "They called you thunder thighs?"

She could only nod.

He rewarded her with a sexy smile. "Then let the thunder roll." He covered her mouth with a hungry kiss and they both fell back on the bed, his body covering hers. He whispered against her lips, "I want to feel your thighs wrapped around me. I want to fear being struck by lightning."

Her heart hammered against her ribs. She couldn't

believe he'd turned a painful nickname into something sexy.

Because that's how she felt. She took the lead, no longer ashamed; she'd worry about how she felt afterwards.

"Make the ground move," he begged. "Make the earth shake. I want to feel every part of you. Make me tremble, baby. Yes... squeeze me like that."

He was being so stupid, she started to giggle.

"Are you laughing at me?"

She nodded.

"I don't care."

And soon she didn't either. She'd lost any feeling of self-consciousness around him. She didn't know how he did it but he didn't make her feel awkward, he was so comfortable in his own skin he made her feel the same. Soon her self-awareness fell away. She wanted to be here with him. If he didn't find her legs and thighs awful, why should she? He made her feel sexy, wild, alive. She wanted this feeling, this moment to last.

Now she knew why she wasn't afraid. She'd met her equal. That's how this felt. In spite of his success and physical beauty she saw a weakness and vulnerability in him that made her feel secure. Safe. He hadn't cruelly teased her; he hadn't dismissed her fears. Instead he'd forced her to face them. She wrapped her arms around his neck and whispered, "Thank you," and she felt him smile.

But she wanted him to do more than smile; she wanted to free him too. To free him from the dark secrets he kept guarded. He wasn't ready yet to reveal all his secrets, but she'd be patient.

Her hands slid down the corded muscles of his back; the dragon dream flashed in her mind when their bodies became one. And she rode this dragon to new heights. She didn't need clouds, her body felt like it was soaring and she reveled in the warmth of his soft flesh as they both went higher and higher...

She might have cried out in ecstasy, she couldn't remember. Her body hummed; her mind empty. All she could do was taste the sweetness of his lips, hear the sound of his breathing, smell the fresh powder scent of his sheets.

They collapsed in each other's arms with languid exhaustion.

In the sudden stillness she said, "You broke the rules you know."

Brett nodded unrepentant. "I know." He grinned. "Can I break them again?"

She met his smile and slid her arm around his neck. "Absolutely."

CHAPTER TWENTY-EIGHT

"I don't want to hear anything else about him."

Corinne stared at Bonnie as they sat across from each other in a popular family friendly restaurant known for great chicken quesadillas and buffalo wings. A humid summer heat had swept through the city, but she suddenly felt ice cold. Her friend's statement had cut through her story about how Brett had made Jason feel useful when he'd invited her son over to play with Alvin and Martha. It had been two months since the workshop and Jason hadn't gotten into anymore fights through the end of the school year and her last weekend visit with him had gone well. He was now on holiday in Italy with Harrison and his family. Jason had sent her a few pictures of his trip, but Bonnie's statement swept that from her mind. "What?"

"This new guy in your life. I'm not interested."

"I've only just started talking about him."

She eyed Corinne's cream colored summer dress. "Is he the reason for your new look?"

"No," Corinne said with a sigh. She was used to Bonnie's dour moods but sometimes it hurt more than others. "And I told you that before."

"Do you really think I'm interested in your sex life?"

"I haven't even mentioned it."

"But you're sleeping with him, aren't you?"

Corinne felt her cheeks burn. "Could you lower your voice?"

Bonnie ignored her. "And you think that means anything? Do you know how easy it is for men to ingratiate themselves into the hearts of single mothers? Don't be surprised if he soon turns cold on you."

"He won't. He's not like that."

"How do you know?"

"I just do."

"It's what you want to believe."

"When you meet him, you'll know what I mean."

Bonnie bit into a pita bite covered in melted cheese. "I have no interest in meeting a man who won't be around for long."

Corinne paused, shocked by her friend's words. "That's low even for you."

"I'm being honest. You really think a good looking guy with a successful business is going to settle for a woman who's living in her parent's house—"

"It's a mother-in-law house."

"With a struggling business—"

"Business has improved."

"And a troubled son—"

"Jason isn't troubled."

"Who can't even decide where he wants to live?"

Corinne rolled her eyes and sniffed. "Well, when you put it like that."

"There's no other way to put it. Didn't Harrison teach you anything?"

"Brett is nothing like him and I'm different now."

"How? Remember when I warned you not to listen to Kyle Conner when he asked you out because it was all to fulfill a bet?"

Corinne swallowed. She hated being reminded of that incident. Hated how quickly she could be transported back to the awkward teenager she'd been. "Yes."

"You listened and avoided being humiliated. The moment I met Harrison I knew it was the same thing. It wasn't for a bet, but he was tired of the usual women he went out with so he chose you. Then what happened? He got bored and ran to the kind of woman he's used to. Brett's no different."

"You don't know that. You haven't even met him."

Bonnie banged the table with the flat of her hand. "I don't have to meet him! I know what he's like and I also know that you're not the woman I remember. I know that right now you're throwing your fabulous new makeover, your sexy new boyfriend, and your amazing business in my face and I'm sick of it!"

Corinne didn't know what to say. One moment Bonnie was reminding her of how bad her life was and the next she was accusing her of bragging about a fabulous life? It didn't make sense. She was used to Bonnie being a buzz kill but something was different this time. This time she sounded angry and bitter. This time her words felt mean.

"I haven't told you anything about my makeover," Corinne said in a low voice. "I went to the Wildfire Spa and showed you my new hairstyle and clothes and that was all. Brett and I haven't been together long."

"Almost three months—"

"It's not like I've been gushing about it every day! I thought you'd be happy when I told you about a referral I got from the workshop that's helping the reputation of my business."

Bonnie's gaze dropped as did her voice. "I feel like your pushing me away."

"I'm here, aren't I?"

She lifted her gaze, her green eyes fierce. "But you're not listening to me. You want to live in this fantasy you've created for yourself and you don't want me to say anything negative against it."

"That's not—"

"But it's going to end and I don't want to be the one to have to put the pieces together like last time."

"I've changed."

Bonnie nodded. "That's the problem. I can't recognize you anymore. I don't know who you are or who you're trying to be."

"For the first time in a long time I'm trying to be myself. I want to wear nice things; I want to be with someone who enjoys my company. I want—"

"I want my friend back," Bonnie cut in. "When you find her, let me know." She stood up and left.

"It was bound to happen," Vivian said with a sigh as she and Corinne finished dinner at a Thai restaurant bursting with the scents of coconut milk and roasted peppers.

Corinne gloomily looked down at her Thai shrimp curry. "No, it wasn't. I know you never liked her but she's been a good friend to me. In high school she—"

Vivian waved her hand with impatience. "But this isn't high school anymore. My God you're not some pimply sixteen year old with a bad perm."

"I never had a perm."

"You know what I mean. You've held on to her out of guilt and loyalty. You outgrew that friendship years ago."

"No, she helped me through my divorce."

"How many times did she remind you that marrying Harrison was a mistake?"

Corinne poked a shrimp with her fork. "But she was right."

"She didn't have to keep telling you so."

"She was trying to protect me. Harrison was out of my league as much as Brett is."

"That's bullshit."

Corinne stared at her friend surprised. "What?"

"You heard me. You and Harrison made a great couple. The marriage may not have lasted but it wasn't because he was so much better than you. What kind of friend would even think that? When I met you, you were one of the top people working at the event planning agency. Everyone was impressed by you. You turned heads. It's no surprise someone like Harrison would take notice."

"And then he got bored of me."

"What if you did nothing wrong? What if in the end it just wasn't a good fit? What then? All I'm saying is that you're living like everything bad that happens is your fault. But sometimes bad things just happen. Marriages end. Careers stall. All you can do is find a way to get through it. That's what life is about. Bonnie may have been a good friend once, but someone who can never be happy for you is not someone you want to keep around forever."

For a moment Corinne felt like curling up into a ball.

Vivian's words rang true, but Corinne still felt a loss. The ending of a friendship was not an easy thing. She wondered if she had bragged about the changes in her life. Had she made Bonnie feel uncomfortable? But Vivian hadn't seen it that way. Vivian cheered her on. Had she been holding on to the comfortable and safe? Had she outgrown Bonnie?

"You're too small," Brett had once told her as they sat together on a bench by the side of a pond, watching ducks swim pass as the sun slowly set in the distance. She'd shared how sometimes she was overlooked when she went to business events and was working on being bolder.

"I'm not small. I'm average height and—"

He shook his head. "I don't mean your stature. I mean the way you move. The way you sit and stand. Ever wonder why I push your shoulders back or lift up your chin?"

"Because you're being annoying?"

A quick grin curved the corner of his mouth. "No, it's because you don't know how to take up space."

"Take up space?"

"As a dancer I learned the importance of expansion and contraction. As children we dart through life, we spin around we raise our hands high, swing through the air. But as we grow older I've noticed that most people's bodies tend to contract. We round our shoulders, shorten our steps. It's important to fight against those limitations so that we are always expanding."

"Is that why you're always moving?"

"One of the reasons." He squeezed her shoulder. "But we're not talking about me, we're talking about you. Learn to keep your back straight, your head high, keep your gaze forward not down. Move as though you belong because you do. Enter a room as if you're meant to be there. When you get a chance, raise your hands above your head, rest your arm the length of a couch. Stretch your legs out in front of you every once in a while. Get in the habit of expanding your body through movement. There's a lot more to you than you think."

At first she'd found his advice a little too simplistic, but when she entered a meeting with a prospective client with her head high and her movements more lucid, she felt a renewed energy. When she'd met Bonnie at the restaurant, she hadn't scurried to the table the waiter had showed them and sat hunched over her food as she usually did. Instead, she mimicked Brett's powerful, yet casual gait as she followed the waiter and then sat with her back straight. Not only had the waiter seemed to have been more attentive than usual, she felt great.

Bonnie was right, she wasn't the woman she used to be.

After her dinner with Vivian, Connie went home and sat on her bed. She held out the third pair of stockings: The animal print that Brett had so admired. The ones she now considered her favorite pair. She privately thought of herself as a lioness. Skilled, powerful and beautiful.

She would no longer tremble at the sound of a drumbeat and think of herself as 'thunder thighs'. She had beautiful, sexy thighs and full hips and she claimed them both with pride.

It still surprised her how Brett had turned her flaw into an asset. She set the stockings down and rested her hands on her hips. No, that was wrong. She'd finally realized her body wasn't flawed. She had nothing to be ashamed of. No matter what happened with her relationship with Brett, the pleasure they'd shared had shown her that she was perfectly imperfect. She had that to hold on to. But she wouldn't hold onto him too tightly, she didn't want to give him a reason to push her away.

She let her hands fall to her lap. She thought losing Bonnie would hurt more, but she was surprised to feel relieved. That was the part that scared her the most. She felt relieved that if things didn't work out with Brett she wouldn't have to have someone constantly reminding her that she'd made a mistake. She felt relieved that she could be happy, even if what they had was just for a little while. She wanted to enjoy this moment. She wouldn't settle for a friendship that no longer suited her.

But she would settle for a man who could leave her too one day.

CHAPTER TWENTY-NINE

He was going to lose her. Brett didn't know how but he sensed that he would. He slid his forefinger down Corinne's bare arm as she lay next to him in bed. Although she had her back to him, he knew she wasn't sleeping.

But she seemed to be keeping him at a distance. He knew he was getting too close, wanting too much, but he couldn't help himself. He wondered if there was something about him that scared her; that made her wary because he sensed it in her touch. She was a wonderful lover, but since their first night, she'd become more cautious.

Her touches were light, like a spring breeze or snow falling on an upturned palm, something one could only hold in memory. He wondered if that represented her. If she was someone he only imagined he could grasp, but who remained out of reach. Someone who would haunt him years later like a ghost.

He didn't need another ghost.

Perhaps he deserved it. He hadn't been completely honest with her about who he was. Who he used to be. He wasn't sure he should risk getting any closer than he already had. There was danger there, he knew it, he danced and toyed with it, but if he wasn't careful it would grab a hold of him and drag him under.

But he didn't care when he knew he should. His mother's visit the other day had warned him. To his regret, Corinne had been forced to meet her sooner than he'd wanted when his mother had invited herself to lunch the same day Corinne had spent the night. They'd planned on a lazy day indoors when his mother had shown up. Their meeting had gone as poorly as he'd thought it would and several days later his mother was eager to tell him so.

"You like her too much," she said as she sat at his kitchen table with a hot cup of Earl Grey. She'd come by to drop off a hat and scarf his father had knitted for Corinne and Jason and Brett hadn't been able to convince her to leave.

"What?"

"You always look ridiculous when you're in love. You would have thought Delaney would have taught you that lesson."

Brett scratched his chin irritated. "I like her. I'm not in love."

His mother sent him a steady look as she took a sip of her tea. "Good. She's not right for you, you know."

He sighed. He didn't need to ask her why she thought

so; his mother was never ungenerous with her opinions. She'd let him know.

"She's weak," his mother said not disappointing him. "I actually saw her hand tremble when she was eating. Can you imagine that?"

"Hmm."

"Although you could always use that in your favor, but I don't want a mouse for a daughter-in-law. In a few years the charm would become tedious."

"She's stronger than you think."

His mother's eyebrows shot up. "Is she now?"

"Yes."

"So she knows how you fell apart after—"

"She doesn't need to know that yet." He glanced at Alvin who had come into the kitchen to drink from his water bowl.

His mother studied Brett with a knowing look. "Because you're afraid she can't handle it?"

He kept his gaze on Alvin, wishing his mother far away. "No." He turned back to her and said in an encouraging tone. "Now if you'll just finish your tea—"

She narrowed her eyes. "You lied to me."

"What?"

"You are in love with her."

He flinched and shook his head before he glanced at the fridge. "I told you I'm not."

"But you can hardly look at me. Does she know?"

Brett sat back in his chair and took a deep breath before he shifted his gaze to her face. He steeled himself and said in a low voice, "Know what?"

"That you've put your heart on a platter for her to slice in two?"

He blinked, feigning boredom although her every word hurt.

"How many times have I told you to be careful?"

"I said—"

"I know what you said, but you don't know yourself yet. You're being reckless. I know you better than you know yourself. Your father told me you're driving more. That's good, but don't push yourself trying to prove yourself like you did with the other one."

"I'm taking things slowly."

"Good because she'll break your heart and leave you in pieces and if you're not careful you'll foolishly let her just like—"

"Enough."

But his mother's words still echoed, long after she'd left his house. They echoed and haunted him.

Especially at times when Corinne was unusually quiet like this.

Their evening had been nice but he sensed something was wrong. There was something she wasn't telling him. Had she sensed something else about him? Had she realized he wasn't as strong as she thought? He'd been careful to keep that hidden. He didn't want to lose her. "What's bothering you?" He felt her stiffen before she said, "I'm fine." She quickly turned to him before he could say anything and snapped her fingers. "Oh, yes, that's right. I keep forgetting to check." She sat up and leaned towards him.

He leaned back. "Check?"

"Yes, I have to count."

"Count what?"

"Your tattoos."

"But I only have—"

She pressed a finger against his lips. "Shh...I want to discover this on my own. Now I know about the one on your neck." She let her gaze fall to a tattoo on his right upper arm. "Is this a spider?"

"Yes."

"I'm surprised it's not a lion."

"I liked this better."

She trailed her finger down his arm. "It's very beautifully done. Trailing down your arm and it has a little face. Is it Anansi?"

"Who?"

"You don't know about Anansi the Spider? A trickster?"

He shook his head.

"Do you have a special appreciation for arachnids?"

"No."

"Then what's the spider represent?" She peered closer. "Wait, does this spider have lashes?"

Brett pushed the bed sheets aside ready to stand. "Hungry?"

Corinne grabbed his arm before he could get out of bed. "No. Tell me about the spider."

He bit his lip suddenly shy. "I can't tell you."

"Why not?"

"Just because."

"Really?"

"Only the woman who inked this knows."

"You got inked by a woman? Are you trying to make me jealous? Is it a secret between you two? A code? You have the spider and she has the web?"

He laughed. "It's nothing like that."

"Then tell me."

He closed his eyes and rested against the headboard. "You'll be the only other person who knows the truth."

"I promise not to tell anyone."

"No." He slid underneath the covers and turned away from her.

She rested her chin on his arm. "Pleaseee."

He sent her a long, considering look over his shoulder, before he turned his head and mumbled something into his pillow.

"What?"

He lay on his back and stared up at the ceiling. "I said it's Charlotte."

"The spider is named Charlotte?"

He nodded. "Yes, like in the kid's story."

She frowned. "Kid's story?"

He threw an arm over his eyes and groaned. "Great. She's never heard of it. She's got a seven year old and she'd never heard of the story." He let his arm fall to the bed. "Forget I said anything."

"Okay." She chewed her lower lip. "Unless you're talking about *the* Charlotte from the wonderful book *Charlotte's Web*? The smart and courageous spider who saved her friend Wilbur the pig from the—"

He covered her mouth. "Don't say it."

She removed his hand. "Where's Papa going with

that axe?" Corinne said, reciting the first line from the book.

Brett glared at her.

She shrugged. "Sorry, couldn't help myself." She peered closer at his tattoo. "Yes, it is Charlotte. I see the little details. I loved that story! I read it so many times. Jason loves it too. Did you cry when she died? I bet you did."

He blinked.

She grinned. "I bet you cried buckets."

He narrowed his eyes; she laughed.

"Don't worry. I did too." She kissed the image. "I didn't realize my boyfriend was so romantic."

"Romantic?"

She nodded then looked away and he saw a sad expression pass over her face.

"What's wrong?"

She paused before she said, "I just lost a friend."

His gaze grew serious. "I'm sorry. How old?"

"No, no, she didn't die," Corinne said with a guilty laugh. "I said that wrong. She—we broke up. I've known her since high school so it's been a blow. It's hard to lose a friend."

"Yes." Brett lifted his hand and tenderly touched her cheek. His face spread into a slow smile. "But now you have a new one." He tapped the picture on his upper arm. "You're the only girlfriend I've ever told about this. Want to know why I chose her?"

She nodded.

"Because she's a true friend and I know how important they are."

"That is so sweet."

He frowned. "I wasn't trying to be sweet."

"I didn't know you were such a softie."

He shook his head. "I'm not."

She pulled the bedsheets back and looked over the rest of him. "Will I find a picture of a very hungry caterpillar, Stuart Little or a dancing pig perhaps?" She paused when she looked down his torso and then looked at his legs. "Where are the other ones?"

"That's what I wanted to tell you. I only have two."

Corinne sighed with feigned disappointment. "Only two?"

"Yes. Go to sleep." He closed his eyes. He didn't know why he'd told her the truth about his spider tattoo. He could have lied. It was something she had over him now. It meant a level of trust he wasn't used to giving anymore. But seeing her smile had been worth it. His mother was right, he was in deep trouble.

CHAPTER THIRTY

AND IT DIDN'T GET BETTER when Delaney showed up at his house. He'd carelessly opened the front door that summer evening thinking it was Corinne. They were going to order food and watch a movie. But instead of Corinne's bright friendly grin he was greeted by an attractive brown-skinned woman dressed in a black lace blouse and jeans and high heels. Her cool brown eyes met his.

He blinked at the sight of her, shocked that she could still affect him.

How could it still hurt to see her? How could the wounds from so many years ago still feel so fresh?

"What are you doing here?"

"Would you believe me if I said I was in the neighborhood?" she said with a grin.

"I wouldn't believe you if you said it was raining outside."

Delaney glanced behind her at the light drizzle

beating against her red Mini Cooper. She turned back to him and sighed. "When are you going to forgive me?"

"What do you want?"

"You know it's not healthy— Wait!" she said when he started to close the door. "I really need your help. There are a few things—"

"No."

"I just need—"

"I don't care what you need. If you're on some assignment from your therapist consider it a failure and go."

"Poor Brett. You're still in love with me," she said then she touched his cheek in a way he wished Corinne would and, to his shame, he let her before he pushed her hand away. "Go home."

"You wouldn't be so angry if you weren't."

"I'm angry because you're wasting my time."

She sniffed. "Yes, you and your precious time."

"Exactly and I'm expecting someone soon so—"

Delaney lifted a finely arched eyebrow. "Does she know about me? About you?"

"Goodbye." He began to close the door.

"Or am I still a ghost? You certainly are to me."

Her words made him pause. He pulled her inside and closed the door. He wanted to get rid of her before Corinne arrived and knew she wouldn't go until she got her way. She'd stay and approach Corinne alone if he let her and he couldn't allow that. "What do you want?"

"I was wrong," she said her gaze pleading for understanding. "I realize how much now."

Brett folded his arms. "I'm happy for you."

"I made a lot of mistakes. I can't apologize enough and—"

Brett ground the words through clenched teeth. "What. Do. You. Want?"

"Gran doesn't know about our breakup—"

"Impossible. It's been years."

Delaney wrung her hands looking guilty. "I sorta told her we'd gotten back together. She liked you so much and she's not well. If you could just visit her and let us pretend for one day that we're still together it would mean the world to her. She still talks about you. That's all I ask."

His hands fell to his hips. "No."

"She's dying Brett. She has a couple months left, maybe. It's not long." Delaney swallowed. "You two were so close."

He lowered his gaze, feeling his resolve weakening. "I can't."

"Just one visit. You know our canceled wedding hurt her more than anyone. She was looking forward to it. It was going to be the first time she ever—"

Brett shook his head. "I don't care." But he did. Too much. He swore. "I can't."

"I wouldn't be here if I wasn't desperate."

He opened the door. "You need to go."

"You know how to reach me if you change your mind. Don't punish her because of me." Delaney grabbed his hand, her grip urgent and familiar. "Please. I'll never ask for anything else."

"I THINK YOU SHOULD DO IT," Corinne said. They sat on the couch with a half eaten veggie pizza sitting on the coffee table in front of them. Brett had been too distracted to watch a movie and instead had told her about Delaney's visit.

He looked at her surprised. "Really?"

Corinne nodded. "If she's dying and it would make her happy..."

Brett leaned his head back and groaned. "I can't believe my girlfriend agrees with my ex-girlfriend about a plan to lie to her grandmother that we're still a couple."

"You told me that it's just one visit."

He lifted his head. "What if she gets better?"

"Then we should find a way to bottle you up as a miracle cure for those on the verge of death."

"I'm serious."

"You don't think she's dying?"

He sighed. "I don't think Delaney would make that up, but I've learned not to always trust her."

"Did you like her?"

He paused. "Actually, I loved her," he said in a quiet voice. "I thought I was going to marry her."

Corinne shook her head. "Not Delaney. I meant her grandmother."

Brett felt his face burn, he'd revealed too much. "Oh, right. Yes, I did like her."

"Then there's nothing wrong with a last goodbye, right?"

A last goodbye. *You know how much our canceled wedding had hurt her...she was looking forward to it...* He rubbed his chin as an idea slowly grew in his mind. He did want to see Delaney's grandmother again and he wanted to make up for a chance she'd missed.

"What's that look for?" Corinne asked, studying his face. "Are you going to do it?"

"No, I have a better idea, but I need you to do me a favor."

CHAPTER THIRTY-ONE

SOMEHOW SHE WASN'T SURPRISED that cancer would take her. Ruth Hayson had reached her eighty-first year the hard way. The second eldest of seven children with a mother who was put in a facility when she was eleven and a father who died when she was fifteen, she'd spent most of her life inside one factory or another all along the south and east coast. Every day had been a hardship, first caring for her brothers and sisters and then the man she finally married. He was a good man, but offered her few tender words or feelings. She liked pretty things although she was never able to afford them.

So she lived through her grandchildren. Their fancy education and fine clothes made all her hardship worth it. They'd gotten a future she'd dreamed for them. But she still wished she'd been able to have a little prettiness before her time on Earth came to an end. Her children thought the tiny bouquet she kept by her bedside was foolish, as was the soft peach comforter she'd saved up for. She'd asked them to buy something similar two birth-days ago, but her son had gotten her a silly cell phone instead, telling her it was more useful. Her family was always treating her to useful, practical things. They never listened to what she truly wanted. Like scented candles and nice, frilly curtains to put on the windows to match the decorative comforter, something to add beauty inside her room. She knew she wouldn't be leaving the nursing facility alive, she wished it could have been a little pret-tier. She sat in her armchair and let her gaze sweep over the dull room and sighed. She turned when she heard a knock on the door. She saw one of the nurses, a friendly woman from some African country whose name she kept forgetting, walk in with a big friendly smile. "Ms. Hayson, you have a visitor."

Before she could ask who, a man walked in. She hadn't seen him in so long she wondered if she had fallen asleep and was dreaming. "Brett?"

He walked over and kissed her on the cheek, and for a moment she was greeted by the scent of tangerine and cedar, the soft touch of his lips made her skin feel young again. "It's been a while," he said, "but I can finally keep my promise."

She frowned, confused. "Promise?"

"Yes." He turned. He was leaving and she felt her heart break a little. "No, don't go, please. Stay awhile longer."

He sent her a secretive look. "I'm not going anywhere. I'll see you soon."

But before she could ask more questions one of the nursing assistants came in holding a silver gown and another followed with a pair of shoes and a scarf followed by a third pushing a hair and makeup trolley. "What's going on?"

The first nurse beamed. "You're going to have an evening you won't forget."

Ruth became more certain she was dreaming when they helped her into the lovely silk dress, she'd never had such beautiful soft fabric touch her skin. Then they styled her wig and did her makeup before they added a sparkling rhinestone tiara.

When they rolled her wheelchair into the recreation room, where the residents usually did activities and listened to guest speakers, Ruth stared around in wonder. The room had been transformed into an elegant ballroom with soft lights and silver streamers, music filtered through the speakers and she turned to see a DJ on the stage. Finally her gaze fell to a round table covered in a white tablecloth where a setting of two silver lined plates and a single red rose sat waiting.

Brett walked up to her and held out his hand. "Tonight I will make your dream come true," he said and she felt tears in her eyes because she'd let that dream die.

Beauty. He'd remembered she'd always wanted a little beauty in her life.

She'd told him years ago that she'd always wanted a night like this. A night wearing beautiful clothes and plenty of food to eat. She'd wanted to dance in the arms of a handsome man and Brett had promised that on his wedding day he'd treat her like a queen.

His wedding hadn't happened. Ruth hadn't been too surprised. She hadn't thought her granddaughter the best match for him. Ruth had met him several years ago at a local gym when she was taking a senior dance class. He'd been friends with their instructor and would drop by occasionally when he was in town and cheer them on. He'd been fun and friendly.

Delaney had put her hooks into him the moment Ruth had introduced them one day when her granddaughter had come to pick her up. Ruth loved her blood, but knew Delaney only saw a handsome, ambitious young man with the potential to look good by her side and make her happy. She didn't see the tender, loving man he truly was. She had a selfish streak and wasn't a good match for him. It still hurt Ruth how right she'd been.

She never thought she'd see him again, but here he was remembering his promise despite all the pain he'd suffered. Still the tender, loving man she'd remembered. She could hardly see him through her tears.

He handed her some tissues. "Don't cry."

She wiped her eyes. "This is too much. You didn't have to do all this."

"A promise is a promise."

"So...it's true? You're back with Delaney?"

He hesitated before he said, "No."

Ruth sighed in relief. "That's good. Have you finally forgiven yourself?" she whispered. "Are you happy now?"

She saw a touch of sadness enter his gaze before it disappeared. He lifted her to her feet, she could walk, not long distances, but he made her forget that. He made her feel as light as a feather, thirty years younger and more beautiful than she'd ever been. "At this moment, more than you can imagine," he said and then they danced.

CORINNE WATCHED Brett and Ruth from a distance, blinking back tears. The image of a strapping younger man so tenderly dancing around a room with an older woman with a smile so bright it could compete with the sun, made all the quick planning and rushing about she'd had to do in the last two weeks worth it.

It was one of the most important events she'd ever managed to pull off. At that moment she realized she wanted to do more events like this. Find more ways to make people's wishes come true. She'd found a new mission and focus. She was ready to take Baylor Events into a whole new direction.

CHAPTER THIRTY-TWO

BRETT LOOKED at the unfamiliar number that popped up on the screen of his cell phone as he hurried his way up the metro station escalator, already feeling the cold breath of an October breeze and smelling the scent of rain from an overnight rainfall. He'd finished a meeting with one of his division managers and was heading to his office to finalize a new property management contract. He wanted to wrap up that Friday early, so that he could be ready for his weekend with Corinne. Since they'd surprised Mrs. Hayson, Corinne had been busy restructuring her business (she'd already gotten two new clients and peppered him with questions eager for his input) and he thought she deserved a break.

He also knew it was the first weekend he'd have alone with her since Jason had started living with her again full-time in September. He was scheduled to see his father this weekend. For weeks Corinne had been excited and nervous about her son staying with her and Brett wanted to know how she'd adjusted to having her son living back with her again after a six month break.

With Jason more fully in her life, Brett wouldn't get to spend as much impromptu alone time with her as he had before, but it surprised him that he didn't care. He liked Jason and every time they had gotten together over the past several months—they'd gone to the zoo, hiking, biking, the museum, the movies—he felt that the kid liked him too. Jason didn't seem as angry as he'd been when Brett had first met him, although he sensed there was still times when he caught an odd expression cross the boy's face that he couldn't read. But Brett didn't want to worry too much; Jason had made a big improvement.

Brett frowned at his ringing phone and thought of ignoring the unfamiliar caller then decided against it. "Lattimore."

"Hello, yes," said an uncertain female voice. "My name is Regina and I have your son with me."

"Sorry, you have the wrong number." He disconnected and put the phone away. It rang again. He sighed when he saw the same number. He answered and said, "Still the wrong—"

"He seems pretty insistent that he talk to you." Seconds later a young boy's voice came on the line. "Hi, Dad. It's me, Jason."

Brett stumbled when he reached the top of the escalator. Dad? Wait...what?

"Could you come pick me up?"

His heart went cold. Jason hadn't called his mother or father. He'd called him. Something was very wrong. He turned to head back down the escalator, calculating how long it would take him to get to the metro station where he'd parked his car. "Give me the address. I'll be right there."

Nearly an hour later Brett saw how wrong things were when he drove up to a brick house and Jason, his clothes covered in grass and mud, came rushing out the front door, carrying his backpack. Brett parked and got out of his BMW, but before he could say anything, Jason said, "Thanks, Dad," and jumped into the backseat.

A worried looking woman with bouncy black curls came up to Brett and said, "I was walking my dog and saw him roaming the neighborhood, I asked him if he was lost or if he went to the local school and he said no. I don't know if he got into a fight or what. He wouldn't say much, just wanted me to call you."

Brett glanced at the silver car and saw Jason with his head down. Why Jason had wanted to call him didn't make sense. He turned back to the woman and shook her hand. "Thanks for everything," he said then got in the driver's seat and pulled out of the driveway. Once the car was a good distance away from the woman's house he pulled over to the side and parked. He turned to Jason and said, "You're supposed to be in school. What happened?"

"I can't go back," Jason said near tears.

"Why? Did someone do this to you?"

He hung his head and the tears fell.

"I'm not angry. I'm worried. Tell me what happened."

He sniffed. "You'll laugh."

"I won't laugh."

"I went to use the bathroom b-but I didn't make it. I didn't want anyone to know so I ran away."

"How did you get so dirty?"

"I rolled on the ground."

"Why?"

"To get muddy," he said simply.

Brett blinked not understanding the logic. "Why did you want to get muddy?"

"'Cause I messed up my pants, I thought if I messed up my clothes too..."

"No one could tell you had an accident?" Brett finally guessed.

He nodded.

Brett scratched his head and nodded as well. He could see some rationale in that. "Fine. I get it. First let me drive to the school to let them know you're okay and—"

Jason quickly shook his head. "You don't have to do that."

"Of course I do. Your teacher—"

"I didn't go to class today."

"What?"

"Grandma dropped me off and I went inside and that's when I...that's when it happened."

Brett glanced at the time, it was nearly twelve. "You've been out of school all this time?"

He nodded.

"Okay, we have to tell your mom—"

"No, she'll kill me. Dad will too. Please I gotta stay with you until school ends."

"I have to call one of your parents. I won't let you get

into trouble," he said quickly when the boy's eyes widened in fear. "We'll get you showered and changed as if nothing happened. All right?"

He nodded.

BRETT CALLED Corinne while Jason was in the shower.

"What do you mean he's at your place? And why do you need a change of clothes? Did he get into another fight? Why didn't they call me?"

"It's a long story and I'll explain later. I just wanted you to know that he's not in school and I'm washing his clothes, but drying may take a while and you told me his father was supposed to pick him up today so you'd better let him know there's been a change of plans."

"But—"

"He's safe. There's nothing to worry about."

"I'll be over as soon as I can."

Brett found a grey knitted sweater for Jason to wear while his clothes got cleaned then parked him in front of the TV. Brett tugged on the collar of his shirt, feeling sweat slide down the back of his neck. Driving Jason had been a little more nerve-wracking than he'd expected it to be. He had to calm down. He heard the ding of the washer and quickly put the boy's clothes in the dryer. "I'm going to take a quick shower," he told Jason who was playing with Martha on the ground, "You know not to open the door to anyone, right?"

Jason nodded.

In the shower, Brett let the water rush over his body

while he took a few steady breaths, to keep his body from shaking. He was okay. Everything was fine. He'd done what he'd had to. He'd done the right thing. Maybe he'd finally recovered. He could start leaving his past behind. He closed his eyes and lifted his face up, letting the water cascade over him. Hope. He could finally hope.

He stepped out of the shower and started to towel dry when he heard the doorbell. Damn, he must have been in the shower longer than he'd thought. He quickly wrapped the towel around his waist and hurried down the stairs. "That must be your mother," he shouted to Jason as he headed to the front door.

But when he opened it, Corinne wasn't standing there.

A man was.

A man whose dark gaze swept over Brett's towel clad body then shifted to the little boy dressed only in a man's sweater, who stood silently behind him. "What the hell is going on?"

"It's not—" A fist to the jaw stopped Brett's words.

"Dad no!"

"You sick bastard," Harrison said and rushed at him.

Brett managed to stop the second attack. But the man's rage was more than he'd expected. Harrison got him in the side with a well placed punch before Brett was able to shove him against the wall. He pressed his forearm against Harrison's neck and subdued him. "Take a deep breath."

"I'll kill you."

"Not if you pass out and with one tiny squeeze I can make sure of that. Now take a deep breath."

"Dad please," Jason begged.

He did.

"Another one."

"Let me—"

"Now."

He did.

They heard the ding of the dryer announcing its cycle had ended.

"It's okay, Jason," Brett said. "Go get your clothes from the dryer."

Jason looked to his father for guidance and Harrison gave a brief nod. Jason looked at the two men uncertain before he left the hall.

CHAPTER THIRTY-THREE

Their eyes met in combat.

Brett released his hold and took a step back. He held up his hand when Harrison opened his mouth. "Before you traumatize your son even more," Brett said in a low voice. "I want you to look at him. Really look at him. Does he look like he's been hurt in anyway? Mistreated? Primed? I don't know what kind of man you think I am, but I don't prey on children. I've been with Corinne for a few months now and I've looked after your son several times. He's been to my house to play with my cats, he knows my father, and he, Corinne and I have had innocent fun together. So when he called me, I came running."

"Why the hell would he call you? Corinne told me he was here."

"I don't know that yet, but right now you have a choice to make. A choice to steal your son's innocence away from him; to teach him to not trust his instincts *or* that it's okay to ask for help when you need it.

"Also, what kind of woman do you think his mother is? Do you think she would trust her son with a man who would abuse him? Is that the lesson you're going to teach him today? That every man is a threat? That only his father can judge for him? He took some bad risks and as a parent you can address them, but not like this. Not this way. But just so you know, I haven't touched him. I'd never touch him. He wanted my help and I offered it. That's all."

Harrison's tone remained hard as did his suspicions. "Then why are you in a towel and he's wearing your sweater?"

"I'll tell you after we agree to a simple lie."

Harrison frowned. "A lie?"

"Yes, Jason's going to wonder why you reacted the way you did. You are not going to soil his mind with your suspicions. You're going to tell him something else."

"What?"

Moments later Jason looked at his father with his eyes wide while he, Harrison and Brett sat in the living room. Brett had managed to get a chance to change out of his towel into jeans and a shirt after they'd concocted their story. "You thought Uncle Brett had kidnapped me?"

"Yes," Harrison said, "and I was so worried I over-reacted."

"He'd never do that." Jason turned to Brett. "Tell him."

Brett nodded. "Of course not."

Jason pulled on the sleeve of his shirt uncertain. "He busted your lip good 'cause of me."

Brett shrugged. "Only because I let him."

Harrison stood. "Okay, buddy, time to go."

Jason jumped to his feet. "Uh...first I gotta feed the cats. Right Uncle Brett? I'll do it now...you said we'd do it." He raced to the kitchen. Before Harrison could follow, Brett stopped him and said, "Let me talk to him for a couple minutes, okay? I think it's important."

Harrison took a deep breath before he nodded and sat back down.

Brett walked into the kitchen where he found Jason squatting next to Alvin and Martha's full food bowls.

He pulled out a chair and patted the seat. "Okay, tell me what's going on."

Jason took a seat and looked at him with hope. "Can we keep it a secret?"

"About what happened today at school?"

He nodded.

Brett rubbed his forehead. "You're too young to have secrets."

"I am?"

"Yes. Secrets are only for grownups. So you can't have secrets until you're, I don't know, maybe twenty-five."

"Twenty-five! That old?!"

"That's right because secrets are how you can spot the monsters."

Jason's eyes widened and his voice grew soft. "The monsters?"

"Yes."

He frowned, skeptical. "Monsters aren't real."

"Yes, they are but they hide very well." Brett rested his arms on the table and leaned forward. "They look ordinary like us so that you can't see them. That's how they get you. But you don't have to be afraid because you can spot them."

"I can? How?"

"Anytime an adult asks you to keep a secret they're monsters. Good adults know secrets can be dangerous. They can get people hurt or even killed."

"Really?"

"Yes, so if you ask me to keep a secret and I said 'yes' I'd be a monster. Adults and kids can't have secrets. Someone else should always know, at least one other person, whether it's your parents or grandparents or someone your parents trust."

"Mom trusts you."

"Right, so we'll have to tell her."

Jason scrunched his face in displeasure. "Secrets are bad?"

"For kids yes. I told you, it's your weapon to spot the monsters. That's why your father was so scared. He thought I was one. Monsters kidnap children."

Jason sighed. "So I have to tell him too?"

"I'll help you. But what you did today was dangerous. That woman could have been one of the monsters. You went inside her house and we never would have known where you were."

"She had a really friendly dog and I called you right away."

"Yes," Brett said with patience, "and I'm proud of

you, but you can't trust strangers so easily. Next time if something happens, go to the principal or the nurse but stay at school. Understand?"

Jason nodded.

Brett took a deep breath and said in a gentle voice, knowing he had to ask, but dreading it all the same, "Has any adult asked you to keep a secret?"

"No."

He felt the tension within him ease. "Good."

Jason tightened his hand into a fist. "But I'm really afraid of monsters, I even drew a picture. Mom told me they're not real, but—"

"She was trying to protect you, but now you know how to spot them. You don't have to be afraid. If they ask you to keep a secret you tell another adult right away. You can tell your mom and dad I told you this, they may get upset but that's okay."

"You'll get in trouble?"

Brett shrugged. "I'll be fine."

Jason rubbed his hands together. "Can we still be friends?"

"Of course, but why did you call me today and not your parents?"

Jason swung his legs. "Because I can tell you like me. Kids can tell when adults like them."

"Your parents like you too. They love you."

Jason shrugged and shifted his gaze to the floor. "But you still like me, right?"

"Of course."

Jason jumped out of his seat, raced over to him and

hugged him, his tiny arms holding Brett tight. "I love you, Uncle Brett."

Brett was too shocked to move at first then briefly hugged him before he pulled back and said in a gruff voice, "Now go. Your dad's waiting."

Jason smiled at him and left the kitchen.

Brett didn't move. He could feel himself sinking. He could feel the waves of fear threatening to pull him under. Fear that he not only loved Corinne, but he loved her son too. He loved them both and he wished...

But she didn't know. He hadn't told her everything yet. Jason didn't know Brett was a different kind of monster. At least that's how he felt.

Brett pushed himself up from his chair with effort and made his way out of the kitchen.

He followed Harrison and Jason to the door, keeping his right hand in a fist to keep it from shaking. Soon he'd be alone. He was safe when he was alone. Jason opened the door then turned and waved at him; Brett forced a smile and waved back.

Harrison sent him a considering look. "Does Corinne know you're such a good liar?"

Brett met his gaze, determined not to reveal his weakness. "Does she know why you jump to conclusions?"

He cleared his throat. "Fair enough. I owe you an apology."

Brett shook his head. "I'm not sure I'm the one you should be apologizing to."

Harrison narrowed his eyes. "What does that mean?"

Brett wasn't sure how to phrase it, but he sensed

Jason didn't realize how much his parents loved him. But it wasn't his place to tell them. "Never mind."

Harrison opened his mouth to say more, but the sight of Corinne's Honda driving up the driveway stopped him. "I guess this is my time to go," he said.

Brett looked at Corinne as she stepped out of her car and for a second, Brett wished Jason and Harrison weren't leaving, because he was afraid.

He was afraid to be alone with her.

CHAPTER THIRTY-FOUR

"I'm sorry I can't do this."

He looked awful. Corinne had never seen Brett in this state before as he stood by the kitchen counter and poured himself a glass of orange juice. She was used to him being a man in motion, but this time was different. He was shaking. She saw his hand tremble as he raised the glass to his lips.

"What happened?" she asked him, confused by his words. He'd explained the bruise on his face, but nothing else. "I thought you said everything was okay with Jason—"

Brett set the glass down with such clumsiness that he spilled some of the juice. "Everything is fine with him." He grabbed a dish towel and cleaned up the spill. "I-it's me. I-I can't do this." He turned to her the dishtowel gripped in his shaking fist. "I'm sorry. I shouldn't have let you believe I could."

"Brett," Corinne said in a tender voice. "Sit down. You're shaking so much it's scaring me."

He folded his arms, but it seemed to make the shaking worse. "I know and I'm sorry. I hate you seeing me like this."

"Brett—"

He closed his eyes. "I can't do this. I can't see you anymore."

Corinne walked towards him then stopped, afraid to get too close. "What happened beside Harrison hitting you? What did Jason do? What did I do?"

Brett opened his eyes and held her gaze. "He didn't do anything. It's me." He took a few steps forward and collapsed in one of the chairs. "You can't trust me. I can't trust myself. I don't deserve this."

"Why not?"

He rubbed his forehead-back and forth, forth and back—in a manic way that frightened her. When he spoke, his voice was filled with pain. "Because I killed my best friend."

Corinne stared at him. "What?"

"Years ago we were both living our dream as dancers in New York. We'd appeared in music videos, stage performances. We were hungry and young when we'd first met at an audition. He got chosen for the production; I didn't, but that didn't stop us from becoming fast friends. He could jump and leap through the air like a rocket, a powerful, amazing performer. For years we felt the world was ours until..." Brett took a deep breath. "Until one rainy night." He briefly covered his eyes with his trembling hand before he let it fall to the table. "We were driving down here to visit family and...the roads were wet, a deer came out of nowhere and I swerved to avoid it. The car spun out of control and we slammed into a tree. I wasn't badly injured; a couple of bruises and scratches, but Tyrone shattered his leg.

"No amount of surgery could get his body to respond the way it once had. He couldn't leap and spin with the force he used to. I tried to help him adjust, he was still able to work, but that wasn't enough. He never accepted that he couldn't dance the way he used to. He pushed himself to exhaustion and his family worried about him. I did too. He never said it, but part of him blamed me and I blamed myself. I thought of ways I could help. I knew dance couldn't be his only future so...

"I'd always had a knack for real estate and housing. When I was young I helped an uncle fix up properties and make repairs. After the accident I bought a cheap duplex and lived on one side and rented the other. I made enough to put a down payment on another property, then another. I was soon getting requests from others to help them manage their properties, deal with tenants who got locked out or cleaning up clumps of hair clogging drains.

"I created Quest and brought Tyrone on board and paid him well. It was supposed to symbolize that we were on another journey...but it wasn't enough. I didn't see that it wasn't enough. Maybe I didn't want to." Brett swallowed. "Anyway, slowly he started to resent me and whatever help I offered him. I didn't realize how much until I met Delaney. I fell for her hard. I thought she loved me too. Until I caught her in bed with him."

"What?"

Brett held up his hand. "Something in me snapped at that moment. Something vicious and ugly came over me. I can be a grade A asshole and I was. I wanted to hurt Tyrone as much as he'd hurt me. So, I pretended to forgive them but slowly made them pay. I connived a way to get him demoted and slashed his salary even though he needed the money at the time."

"That's understandable. He betrayed you."

"I didn't stop there. I knew how much he cared for Delaney. By that time I didn't care whether I loved her or not. It was only later that I learned she also brought out the worst in me. But at that time all I cared about was revenge. I wanted to show Tyrone that I could have what he couldn't. I made him best man at my wedding, sent him the wedding invitation just for the thrill of it with a picture attached.

"That's when he told me how he really felt. He begged me not to marry her. That he loved her more than he'd ever loved dance. I didn't care. I didn't hear him..." Brett briefly covered his eyes and fell silent.

"What happened?"

Brett looked at her with haunted eyes. "Tyrone killed himself a week before the wedding." He nodded solemnly when Corinne stared at him speechless. "I pushed him too far and I didn't handle it well. I didn't handle it well at all. I cancelled the wedding and I told her why. That I'd used her; that I didn't love her anymore. She called me a killer. She wasn't far from wrong. Tyrone had the last laugh. In one week my life fell apart."

"But that wasn't your fault."

Brett lifted up his sleeve to reveal his Charlotte tattoo. "I wasn't a true friend. I wanted to hurt him and I did. And Delaney saw that because she's as nasty as me. I pretend to be someone else, but—"

Corinne started to reach for him then drew away. "No, that's not—"

"Your son is so precious and for a moment when I had him in my car, the roads were wet and I wondered what would happen if I made a mistake again..."

"It was an accident."

"The car crash yes, but not what happened afterwards. That was on purpose. He blamed me; I let him, but then when he did what he did... I wanted to hurt them both. I used her, toyed with him... I should have let it go. Or forgiven them, especially him. I shouldn't have left him hanging and then shoved my happiness into his pain." He rubbed the back of his neck. "Sometimes I feel so broken that it's hard to breathe. As if I'm made up of shattered glass and every breath cuts me inside, causing me to bleed. I'm a broken man; an ugly man with deep scars. That day when I saw you standing on the metro platform I knew what you were thinking because I've thought it myself. Many times. I can't love you; I can't love your son. Not the way you both deserve." He pushed his chair back and stood.

"Brett—"

"You don't know how much I hate you seeing me like this. I'm ashamed."

"Brett we can—"

"I can't. I'm telling you who I really am. I'm not kind. I'm not good. I'm telling you I can't be what you need."

And she heard him and it angered her. It angered her that he was pushing her away when she'd been so careful. So understanding. She'd let him guard his secrets, but now he'd grown tired of her. Now that Jason was back in her life he didn't want the responsibility. She wasn't fun anymore.

"I thought you were different," she said bitter. "But you're a coward like Harrison. You always get to set the rules. One moment I'm convenient and then I'm not. Don't pretend to be noble. Don't pretend you're pushing me away as some grand gesture of protecting me and my son. You're giving me excuses not reasons. You're protecting yourself because you are—" She squeezed her eyes shut. "I hate you so much right now." She glared at him. "The first time I saw you, I thought you were a heartless, cold bastard and I was right. But you're not only that, you're also cruel."

"Corinne—"

"Cruel enough to let my son trust you. What am I supposed to say to him now? No, don't say anything. This is my fault. I was the foolish one. I knew this wouldn't last. I knew you weren't the one and I lied to myself that you were worth the risk. I was wrong."

She turned and stormed away.

CHAPTER THIRTY-FIVE

She lied.

Over the next several weeks Corinne lied to her son about Brett. She told him Brett was traveling and that was why they couldn't see him. When Jason caught her crying one night, she lied that she had watched a movie that had made her sad.

When he wondered why she'd forgotten to pick up his Halloween costume from the store, she lied and said she'd gotten busy at work. Some nights she dreamed about a dead dragon, a magnificent creature that had once helped her soar into the clouds, now lay still at the mouth of a dark cave, its eyes closed. There was no promise of flight. No promise of ecstasy. She stood and grieved alone.

When Jason asked her why her eyes were puffy and red, she told him she couldn't sleep.

Then one Saturday morning as a December snow

softly fell outside, he replied to one of her lies with something she never wanted to hear again.

"I want to live with Dad."

This time she heard him the first time.

"We agreed that you'd stay with me for six months and then we'd decide."

"No," Jason said his eyes filling his tears. "I want to go now."

"Why? I thought—"

He lowered his head and wiped his tears away with the back of his hand, his voice shaking. "I know you don't like being a mom."

Corinne stared at him utterly astonished. "What?"

"I know because when we moved here you were sad. I was always in the way, you were always wondering what to do with me and then when I left to live with Dad, you got pretty and you got new clothes and met Uncle Brett. But now...now I'm back with you and you're sad again."

She inwardly shuddered; guilt piercing her. She rushed around the table and pulled him into her arms. "Oh, my darling. I am so sorry you ever thought that. It's not true." She drew back and cupped his tear-stained face in her hands. "I *love* being a mom, especially *your* mom. You're the most important person to me. I missed you every day you weren't here. I got new clothes and worked hard at my business because I wanted to make you proud. I wanted you to be proud that I'm your mom."

"I am, Mom," he said, "and I love you." He kissed her on the cheek and hugged her. "But you're still sad."

He was right and the guilt dug deeper. She didn't

want her son to see that. "That's not your fault, it's mine. I'm working on it."

"Uncle Brett said I should draw you a picture. Would you like one?"

She felt her heart twist. "You spoke to Brett?"

He frowned. "Yes, I call him sometimes. Mr. Lattimore too. Why are you looking like that? I didn't do anything wrong, did I? You said I could. You said it was okay."

Her heart pounded. Of course! Jason thought nothing was wrong. Jason didn't know she and Brett had broken up. She'd forgotten about her lies. She felt relieved that Brett hadn't abandoned her son and cut him out of his life the way he had her. She was grateful that Jason wouldn't be hurt, but she was also angry. Like Harrison, Brett had tossed her aside and saved his affection for her son. It was so much easier to dote on a child. But a woman? Was that too much? Of course it was. He couldn't love her. That's what he'd told her.

He couldn't love *her*. But she wouldn't think about that now. She didn't care. She didn't care if Jason visited Brett and his father. They were no longer part of her life and she'd move on. She turned her attention back to Jason and saw him studying her face, unsure. She forced a smile, but as she looked into his serious brown eyes her smile became genuine. "I'd love to get a picture from you," she said. "Something I can hang in my office and think of you."

He jumped up. "I'm going to get started right now."

"Clear your dishes first."

He quickly gathered his plate and utensils and put

them in the sink with a clatter before he dashed out of the room.

Corinne tried not to think about Brett as she washed up the dishes, but he wasn't far from her mind.

She heard the doorbell and frowned. She wasn't in the mood for visitors. She'd told her parents about her breakup, how she was hiding the truth from Jason, and her mother had patted her on the shoulder and said, "What a kerfuffle," before putting on a pot of tea. Since then she'd been plying her with enough buns and biscuits to open a shop.

Corinne opened the front door and stared surprised to see Rania. "You haven't worn your fourth pair yet."

Corinne shook her head. "Did you really need to come to my house to say that?"

"Yes." She pushed past her and walked into the living room.

"Doesn't matter. I'll get to them when I'm ready."

Rania sat and said in a low voice, "What are you waiting for?"

"I really don't need this right now."

"You're so close. You can have all that you want, if you're willing to reach for it and hold on."

Corinne lowered her voice not wanting her son to overhear although his bedroom was a good distance away. "I've already lost Brett."

"And you're going to lose him for good if you don't change."

"Change?" Her voice cracked. "Why would I have to change? He told me to leave."

Rania raised her brows shocked. "Did he really? When?"

"He said he couldn't love me. That he couldn't be with me. That a relationship wouldn't work."

"He said that?"

Corinne rolled her eyes annoyed. "I'm paraphrasing. It's the basic gist."

"But did he tell you to leave? Did he say the words?"

Corinne scowled wondering why Rania was being so particular. She hesitated. "I don't know."

"Think."

The conversation had been so painful she hated to think about it. She hated to see how Brett had been shaking and avoiding her gaze. How he'd said he couldn't love her, how much of a jerk he was, how she'd been afraid to touch him...but...he hadn't told her to leave. Why hadn't she noticed that? "But he wanted me to leave. I could tell."

"Really?"

"He didn't want me to see him. He said he was embarrassed."

"So you left him."

"But he said he—" She stopped horrified. He'd never said he'd wanted her to go.

"In your application you said you preferred lions over dragons. Why is that?"

"Because lions are real."

"But you treated Brett like a dragon. Like a mythical creature out of reach. How long were you willing to let him guard his secrets, like a dragon guards its treasure? Were you ever willing to take the risk to shine a light in his darkness even if that meant he would run away? You didn't want to push him; you didn't want to love him. That's what he knew. That's why you left. He didn't leave you."

She'd left him. She'd walked out on him. How could she have been so blind? She'd acted like a child. Like Jason, she'd seen what she'd wanted to see. She'd become so used to being mistreated, to Harrison's manipulation, that she hadn't seen how different Brett was. He hadn't said he didn't love her, just that he couldn't. She now saw that he was afraid. Afraid that she'd leave him and she had.

She wondered if Tyrone had been like Bonnie; if he hadn't been a true friend at all. What if he'd been jealous of Brett? What if he'd wanted to make him suffer? Wanted to punish him? That's why he'd chosen Delaney of all the woman to betray Brett with. He knew how Brett felt about her. His father had once told her that Brett loved too fully, without restraint and that betrayed love had turned him into someone vengeful. Dangerous. That's what frightened him about himself, so he'd learned to protect himself...and others.

Her pain had made her blind to his fears.

Rania leaned forward. "There are times to let go and times to hold on. What are you going to do now?"

Corinne sighed. Rania was right. It was time for her to change. Time to stop settling for feeling like a victim, to take hold of what she wanted even if it wasn't perfect.

"You really think wearing the final pair of stockings will make a difference?" she said, doubtful.

Rania flashed a mischievous grin. "You haven't really

looked at them, have you? When you do, the answer will come to you." She stood. "Good luck."

"Wait, how did you know he hadn't told me to leave?"

"I didn't."

"And if he had?"

"I would have asked you why you'd listened." Rania folded her arms. "It's not about him Corinne. It's about you. How your actions affect others."

You're more powerful than you think, Brett had once told her. She finally understood what he meant.

Corinne raced to her bedroom and pulled out her final pair of stockings. When she saw its design she started to smile. She understood exactly what Rania meant and knew what to do.

CHAPTER THIRTY-SIX

COLD, *heartless bastard. Cruel.*

Cruel.

Cruel.

Brett lay on his couch, wrapped in a throw, with Martha curled up at his feet and Alvin asleep on his head, purring softly. Corinne was right. She'd seen the truth and been disgusted, just as he thought she would be.

He'd gotten too close. He'd been able to go to work, although he hadn't been able to drive. He hadn't been able to get control of the shaking yet, even at work there had been a number of times clients had noticed his hand trembling and been too polite to say anything.

He heard a knock on the front door and pulled up the throw tighter around him. Alvin shifted his position. Brett hoped whoever was there would take the silence as a hint and go away.

After the sound of the doorbell, he heard a key in

the lock and groaned. It had been a mistake to give his mother a key. He hadn't returned their calls in a while and he'd been prepared for one of them to check in on him. She'd be delighted to see him on the couch like this. He wouldn't fight her. "You're right, Mom," he called out when he heard the front door close. "When she found out who I really am, she stepped on my heart and I let her because I'm weak. You don't have to rub it in."

He heard the sound of her high heels come closer. He closed his eyes. "I wasn't careful. I know. You were right, I was wrong."

He heard Alvin grumble in protest as he was pushed away. He felt a gentle hand on his forehead.

Brett froze. His mother never touched his forehead like that. Even when she suspected he had a fever, she'd just pop a thermometer in his mouth and check the reading. He opened his eyes and blinked twice when he saw black stockings with a spider web pattern. His gaze slowly lifted to a sleek black dress and finally fell on a face he'd foolishly grown to love.

Corinne!

He sat up, frantic. She wasn't supposed to be there. Damn, why was he shaking again? She wasn't supposed to see him like this. "Wh-what are you doing here?"

She sat down beside him, a secretive smile on her lips. "I have something I forgot to tell you."

Hadn't she told him enough? He knew he was cruel. He knew how much he'd hurt her. He knew all his flaws and failings. "I don't—"

"My given name isn't Corinne."

He furrowed his brows. He didn't know why that was important.

"It's Charlotte." She took his hand. "I may not be small and wise and I might get scared and run away, but one thing you can count on is that I will come back. I will always come back to you. You won't be alone."

"But—"

"I was wrong. I didn't hear you and I'm sorry. You're not heartless or cruel anymore than I am."

He shook his head with regret, his voice broke. "I'm a broken man, trying to put himself back together—"

"You don't have to do that," she said with a gentle smile. "You can't go back to the past; you can't try to think of all the ways you could have been someone different. Change who you used to be. You have to become somebody new." She squeezed his hand. "You once told me how we tend to contract our bodies as we get older, but I think we contract our lives too. I did it. I kept my social circle small. I kept thinking about reasons why my marriage broke up, so much so that I didn't even realize how much I was hurting my son by not living in the present, and not looking towards the future." She squeezed his hand tighter. "It's time you expand your life too. You've more than enough made up for the past. It's time to open up and let us in. Let me be in your life and Jason too. Let your life be as big as your heart because that's who you truly are: A man with a tender heart who got it broken."

"But I—"

"I don't care. It's over." She bit her lip. "I said words to you out of anger that I shouldn't have. I'm sorry. The man who helped Mrs. Hayson's dream come true is far from cold or heartless. The man who made up an animal fundraiser so my son could feel needed is far from cruel. He's someone I love."

"I know I scared you when you found out the truth about me," he said in a raw voice.

Corinne shook her head. "No, I was already scared. I was scared that what we had was too good to be true. I expected it to end. You just gave me a reason to run away."

He swallowed. "Why did you come back?"

"Because I'm your Charlotte and I love you. You don't have to be alone anymore."

His body still shook, but she wasn't letting go. He felt the strength of her grip on his hand. It wasn't light, it was grounded. Committed. She wasn't going anywhere. She was staying with him. Staying by him. She accepted him fully.

And in that moment he became a new man. He no longer felt the jagged edges of his regrets and sorrows, instead he felt peace. Joy. Love. He loved her completely and the thought didn't frighten him anymore. It made him feel strong.

He gathered her in his arms and kissed her because he could not tell her with words how much she meant to him. He drew back and took a deep breath. "Can I hire you for another event?"

Corinne blinked, confused by the change in topic. "Okay...what is it?"

"Do you do weddings?"

Corinne's face softened into a smile and the love in

her eyes made him feel at home. "It's not my specialty, but I already have a few ideas..."

TWO YEARS LATER...

Corinne tried to keep sight of Jason's blue knit cap, the one Mr. Lattimore had knitted for him, as her son made his way through the crowded metro platform. He pushed the stroller in front of him as if he were navigating a ship, taking pride in his role as older brother to his younger brother Liam. They were all headed to the Kennedy Center for a performance Jason had seen before and was eager to share with his brother.

Corinne was about to call out to tell Jason to slow down when she spotted her husband, Brett, getting close to the knit cap. Fortunately, seeing him proved much easier and she let her worries subside. He knew how to keep an eye on them.

She looked up at the schedule and saw the train was to arrive soon.

"Are you going to the children's theater?" a voice said behind her. She turned and saw Doris. She hadn't seen her in a while and when she'd asked Doris' daughter about her, when they'd both volunteered for an event at their children's school, she'd told Corinne her mother had been traveling.

"Yes," Corinne said.

"We are too," she said gesturing to her daughter and grandchildren.

"It's good to see you."

Doris beamed. "It's even better to see you. You look happy."

"I am."

"That's good." She tugged on her ear and Corinne noticed that her earring was shaped like stockings.

"Wait, are you—"

"Mom!"

Corinne turned at the sound of her son's voice and saw the train doors were open. She hadn't heard it arrive. In a few seconds the doors would close. She saw Jason frantically waving her forward and then she noticed Brett.

Their eyes met.

She couldn't completely read the expression in his gaze but she saw some uncertainty. She remembered the first time they'd met. How she'd watched the train doors close between them.

She started to run.

It felt good to run towards something.

Her beautiful family.

A beautiful future.

This was not a train she was going to miss. She jumped onboard just as the doors began to close. Brett grabbed her when she stumbled against him.

"That wasn't a good idea," he said, but he sounded relieved and the apprehension that had touched his gaze was gone.

Corinne laughed at his scolding and said with a heart full of joy, "Actually, I think it was one of my best ideas yet."

www.ingramcontent.com/pod-product-compliance
Lightning Source LLC
Chambersburg PA
CBHW050511190726
48284CB00003B/770